THE SECRET OF POODUCK ISLAND

"It came true," he said breathlessly.

The Secret of
Pooduck Island

By ALFRED NOYES

With Drawings By
FLORA NASH DeMUTH

FREDERICK A. STOKES COMPANY
NEW YORK AND PHILADELPHIA

COPYRIGHT, 1943, BY
ALFRED NOYES

Printed in the United States of America

Published August 23, 1943
Second Printing, January 15, 1944

No part of this book may be reproduced
without the written permission
of the publishers.

This book has been designed in accordance with
Government regulations for saving paper during
the war; the bulk has been reduced from cus-
tomary peacetime standards.

To

GEORGE AND CLAIRE WATERMAN

*in memory of many happy
hours at Pooduck Farm
in Maine*

Contents

I

THE SQUIRRELS KEEP HOUSE

I know a cottage on the coast of Maine . . .
Let a jack-pine rustle, and I'm living there again,
In a clearing of the woods where the waves say 'woosh'
And the sea-swallow nests in a wild-rose bush,
And the little wild strawberries redden under foot,
And the woodchuck nibbles at the rose-marie root,
And the fish-hawk over the pine wood wheels,
And the cormorant cries to the barking seals,
Till the Red Man's ghost in a birch-canoe
Dips his paddle and . . .

NOBODY WAS THERE. You might have thought that someone had been singing, and suddenly stopped. But there was nobody. Everything was quite still. There was only the sound of the long sea-

1

wave washing peacefully against the red and gray rocks below.

Only a moment ago, it seemed, somebody had been standing there to listen; somebody standing there to breathe the scent of the sun-warmed pine-needles, and the salt smell of the tawny seaweed as it rose and fell with the clear green water.

The deserted cottage looked as if it were waiting to be remembered. It was backed by a half-circle of pine trees and silver birches. It stood on a little rockbound meadow ledge, overlooking a broad reach of deep-blue sea. In the distance it saw three small pine-tufted islands, where only seagulls and other wild creatures lived. Beyond these was the Atlantic.

But Blueberry Cottage looked far too cheerful to be deserted so early in the fall. It was built of sturdy pine, with a rough-stone chimney and a roof of well-seasoned shingle. In the patch of long grass and ferns around it the bees were still hovering over the wild Michaelmas daisies; and among the rocks, there were all sorts of deliciously scented little shrubs where the rambling foot-wide path went down to the beach. In front of the cottage the sun was flooding the wide verandah. On one of its sun-blistered green tables there was a book with a faded cover. Everything else had been 'put away.' The windows had shutters; and these, apparently, were all made fast.

A song-sparrow piped three plaintive notes where the pines went down to the water. It was too delicious never to have been heard by someone who enjoyed it. It was not the time for bird-song, but it was answered by a remote elfin echo, dying away along the coast. Somebody had listened to that lonely cry, keen and sweet as a pine-needle pricking your heart. But nobody was there now.

From above the cottage there came a soft thud, as though a pine-cone had fallen on the shingled roof. It was followed by another; and then two more, rather lighter than the first two. If there had been any human there, he might have seen, on the ridge of the roof, two red squirrels sitting upright, with their bushy tails erect behind them, and their cocked ears and bright black eyes alert for danger. But they, too, seemed to be sure that everyone had gone away. One of them uttered a light chirrup, and immediately there were two smaller squirrels, one on each side of their parents, in the same attitude, ears cocked and eyes glancing around them with unmistakable delight in the absence of all humans.

There was a further chirrup which, in their own language, undoubtedly meant "do be careful, Grandfather"; and a larger squirrel, whose coat was turning gray, dropped somewhat more heavily onto the roof beside them.

It was no new adventure, for after making quite certain that they would not be disturbed, they all moved quickly to a sheltered corner near the chimney, where Mrs. Squirrel displaced a loose bit of shingling and discovered their private entrance to the house. One more glance around them—to make quite sure that no human was there; and, one by one, they entered. The last to enter cunningly readjusted the loose bit of shingling, so that no hole could be seen even by a wandering sea-gull overhead. Then all was as quiet as before; and, if the human owner of the cottage had returned and walked round the outside of his abode he would have suspected nothing. Nor could he have imagined what was happening within.

2

BLUEBERRY COTTAGE

"QUEER CRITTERS, these humans," said Grandfather Grizzle—for that was the name of the oldest Squirrel—"very queer critters, these humans!"

It was late afternoon of the day on which they had taken possession of Blueberry Cottage; and Grandfather Grizzle sat comfortably cushioned in the ingle-nook of the rough-stone chimney. He glanced, critically, from the Cape Cod lighter on the hearth to the bookshelves on the walls; but on the whole he approved of the winter-quarters which his family had chosen. He especially liked this large central room, which went right up to the roof and had a gallery running the whole way round it, with a trellised balustrade of silver birch logs. The prettiest of stairs, with

another trellised balustrade of silver birch led up to
the gallery. It was this in fact that had settled the
Squirrels' choice. It made them feel quite at home immediately; and nobody who saw the two younger squirrels running upstairs by the silver birch trellis, or
playing hide-and-seek through the even more delightful silver birch trellis of the gallery, could doubt that
the choice was a wise one.

There were bedrooms and bathrooms opening out
of the gallery. But the doors of these were shut, with
one exception, of which we may hear later. The Squirrels were not greatly interested in the others. Nor did
they wish to use the dining and other rooms opening
out of their central hall on the ground floor. They
were very well pleased with this big central room
which, of course, was only dimly lighted, except for a
ray or two which filtered in through a crevice in the
high window shutters at either end. The verandah,
however, might be useful, as it was the one place in
the cottage from which they could keep an eye on the
outside world. But it was shut off from their big central room by a shingled partition and a glass-topped
door.

"Ruff and Curly ought to gnaw a hole through them
shingles," said Grandfather Grizzle. He often deliberately talked in that way because he thought it sounded
'tough' and 'red-blooded.' But, of course, he knew better. They had promised him that this improvement
would be carried out in a day or two; but naturally he

was not to be denied the pleasure of criticizing the absent humans.

"Think of collectin' all that junk," he said, waving a paw at the crowded bookshelves, "and not a nut to be found in the whole house. Not so much as a beech-nut. Queer critters, they are!"

"Not so queer as you think," chuckled Ruff, the elder of the two Squirrel children. He was turning over the pages of an illustrated book of poems, with his eager little forepaws. "Look at this picture!"

It was an illustration of the famous quarrel between a Squirrel and a Mountain; and the Squirrel was re-markably like Grandfather Grizzle. Ruff's sister, Curly, drew near to inspect it; and they both broke into a delicious chirrup of laughter that sounded like beech-nuts falling into a brook.

"It's Grandfather Grizzle to the life," said Ruff, when they had recovered.

Mrs. Squirrel looked up from her domestic duties. She had been industriously tearing a new down cushion apart to make winter bedding for her household. Indeed she never wasted a moment. This was why her husband (who was out in the woods this evening rather later than usual) always called her by the affectionate name of 'Cosy,' though Grizzle—who had no weak sentiment about him—insisted that the name had been suggested by the soft covers that humans used to keep their teapots warm.

Mrs. Squirrel looked over Ruff's shoulder at the picture; and she, too, broke into a laugh that sounded like ripe acorns dropping into a trout-pool.

"It's the spit image of him," she cried.

"Look at it for yourself, Grandfather," chorused Ruff and Curly, lugging the book across the room to the chimney corner.

Grandpapa Grizzle looked at the picture. It was certainly the picture of an elderly squirrel; and all in color, too. Moreover, the whiskers had exactly the disdainful look of his own. This was really why the others had laughed, though they didn't like to say so. Grizzle was obviously surprised at the likeness but he was not so weak as to admit it.

"Pshaw," he sniffed. "I could do better than that myself."

"Why, you've never made a picture in your life," said Mrs. Squirrel.

"Haven't I? What about this?" the old fellow answered, swelling out his chest, and making his bushy tail even more bushy than usual. "What about this?"

"It's magnificent," said Ruff, "but it's not a picture."

"Of course not," said Grizzle. "It's the real thing. That's why I said I could do better."

As nobody could think of any possible answer to that, Mrs. Squirrel suggested that, anyway, the picture might be hung on the wall immediately opposite Grandfather, and perhaps he might come to like it, in time.

Ruff ripped the picture out of the book with the greatest enthusiasm, and jammed it on to a nail, which was already fixed in the wall as though waiting for the very purpose of holding the precious portrait up to Grizzle's offended gaze.

"I don't suppose the humans would like everything we are doing," said Curly, who felt that the nail hadn't altogether improved the picture.

"Well. Tastes differ. There's no fixed standard about these things," replied Mrs. Squirrel.

"Everyone must admit that it can at least be *seen* now," interjected Ruff.

Mrs. Squirrel agreed.

"I never have believed in putting away beautiful things where they can't be seen or used," she said.

Grizzle snorted at this.

"You seem to forget I've lived among the humans that make these things—'artists' is what they call 'em, I believe."

Grandfather Grizzle had actually lived for nearly six months in the chimney of an artist's studio, over at Buffalo Creek; so he was naturally a little proud of his opinions about pictures. Mrs. Squirrel tried to be tactful.

"Of course," she said, "we know that you're a real judge, Grandfather. That's why we hung it on the wall; we wanted to get your honest opinion about it."

Grandfather Grizzle was pleased again but he tried not to show it. He looked at the portrait on the wall for some time, chewing a little plug of acorn with an air of great wisdom. He was really imitating a critic whom he had watched one day through a knot-hole in one of the wooden walls of the studio. But the Squirrel family didn't know this, and they waited almost breathlessly for the judicial decision. At last he broke silence.

"It lacks bultitude," he said.

"Lacks what?" said Curly, while Ruff gave a little sneeze to prevent himself laughing.

"Bultitude," said Grizzle, spitting the plug of acorn into the fireplace.

"I don't believe that's a word at all," said Mrs. Squirrel.

"I never said it was," said Grizzle tartly. "You don't have to use real words when you're talking about Art. Didn't I live in the—er—"

"Chimney," suggested Mrs. Squirrel.

Grandfather froze her with a look.

"*Circles* is the word they use, I believe," he said in a voice like a little buzz saw. "I admit there was often a lot of smoke. But I've lived among 'em; and that's what this picture lacks—*bultitude*. It's what they call a substrackshun. I don't 'spose you'd know what a substrackshun is."

"It's what human children do at school," said Curly. "It's a kind of sum, like this. *If you had three acorns and ate two, how many of them are left?* And the answer is 'none,' because Ruff eats the other one. It's quite easy, if only you don't think about it."

"It means a lot more than that when you're an artist," said Grizzle, taking another acorn out of the little bag at his side and putting it into his mouth. "It means that if anything has anything that makes it look like anything, the artist takes it away. See?"

"I don't *quite*," said Mrs. Squirrel.

"You would if you'd lived in the Circles," said Grizzle. "Let's put it this way. An artist is painting your portrait. Naturally, he don't want it to look like *you*. So if there's anything in your face that does make it look like *you* he takes it away. That's substrackshun. See?"

There was an awe-struck silence for several moments after this. It was broken at last by Ruff, who said rather nervously, "Let's leave it on the wall for a day or two anyway, and see what happens."

"If the humans come back, you'll see what will happen all right," said Grizzle. "I advise you to keep a sharp watch. You can't trust 'em even in winter. They're a queer lot. You should have heard the language that Scots minister, the Reverend Ebenezer Mac-Doodle used over at Blink Bonnie when he came back last summer and found we'd been taking care of his house during his absence. *Where's my gun?* he said. I was up in the woodpecker's hole, in the oak tree, just above the door, and I heard him with my own ears. '*Where's my gun?*' he said, '*I'll blast the leetle deevils out of every tree in the place.'* Now, I'll admit that the blankets Cosy shredded for the winter bedding belonged to the Reverend Ebenezer. But that was no language for a minister; and, after all, he could get more blankets, and squirrels have only one life."

Mrs. Squirrel was quietly ripping another cushion to pieces.

"Murderous, I call it," she said. "I'm glad this isn't a minister's house."

"Have you any idea who the owner may be?" asked Grizzle, somewhat grimly.

Mrs. Squirrel shook her head; but Ruff gave a queer little cough and said, "I heard something about that, last night, from Solo."

"And who the porcupine's whiskers is Solo," said Grizzle.

"The other village boys think he's cracked because he won't shoot us squirrels," said Curly. "But he's much more sensible than most of the humans. He's the only one that can talk to us squirrel children. That's why we call him Solo. His mother calls him that, too. He likes squirrels better than humans. He says that they can do things without thinking about them, while the humans are always thinking about them and can't do them. Ruff and I talked to him in the woods last night. He said this house belonged to a poet, once; but the poet's dead and now it belongs to the poet's children."

"A poet? What's a poet?" said Mrs. Squirrel.

"As far as I could make out, it's something like Solo," said Ruff. "Anyway they never do any harm to squirrels."

"Anyone can see you've never lived in the Circles," said Grizzle, "or you'd know that having a poet in the family ain't no insurance."

"Well," said Ruff, "Solo used to cut wood for that artist down at Buffalo Creek; and looked after the Circles when he was away, too. So he ought to know about it. The artist gave him some old brushes and paints; and taught him how to use them, too. Solo used to watch him all day long. I've seen Solo himself painting when he thought no humans were looking. He says artists like a lot of things that most humans don't like, and squirrels do. So I expect this poet's family will be as pleased as chickadees to find we've taken the down out of their cushions."

"And pulled the picture out of the book, where nobody could see it," said Curly.

"And left the nut-shells in their best bed," said Mrs. Squirrel. "I always say that gives a nice homey feeling."

"Don't trust 'em," said old Grizzle. "Look at that."

He raised his right forepaw, and pointed to a cupboard with a glass front, at the back of the room. There was a twelve-bore gun in it, a rook rifle and several other minor weapons.

"You know what those are," said Grizzle. "Those are their fire-sticks. Humans kill squirrels with 'em. Humans kill birds with 'em. Humans even kill humans

with 'em, by the thousand. I tell you, they're queer
critters, humans. I don't trust 'em."

"I hope Daddy is all right," said Curly, glancing
nervously at the windows and doors.

"There. You've scared the children," said Mrs.
Squirrel, "just as we've settled them into this nice com-
fortable house for the winter. It's really too absurd,
Father."

But she looked a little nervous herself, and decided
not to do any more tearing up of cushions that night.

"I do wish Daddy wouldn't stay out so late," she
said. "I wonder what is keeping him."

At that moment there was a curious whistle at the
door. It was not a bird's whistle. It was not quite a
human whistle either.

Grizzle and Mrs. Squirrel looked at one another.

"It's all right," said Ruff. "It's Solo. It must be important. That's our secret whistle. Look! He's push-
ing the window up."

A little side window, of which the broken catch had
been overlooked by the humans, went up with a rattle;
and, framed in the dark opening, a strange face appeared.

It was indeed a very strange face. You couldn't say
it was young; nor could you say it was old. It might
have been almost any age. It might have belonged to
a boy of sixteen, or, by its tanned weatherbeaten skin,
to a sailor who had spent years before the mast. It was
wrinkled, but so is a young pine tree; and its dark eyes

were large and moist like the eyes of a young stag; and tonight they looked as startled and anxious as if he thought the hunters were on his track. The Squirrel family knew that look. It usually meant that humans were in the neighborhood. It was a minute or so before they realized that Solo's anxiety was for the Squirrel family, not for himself, and that he was trying to break some bad news to them.

"Ssh," he said, putting a finger to his lips. "They're not far away. There's nothing to frighten you. But your Daddy's been hurt. I've brought him back. He'll be all right in a day or two."

With this, he carefully lifted a bundle through the window, and laid it down gently on the floor. He then closed the shutters and cautiously lit a stump of candle, which showed that the bundle was Mr. Squirrel, wrapped up in Solo's woolen jersey, and looking rather weak and ill. Cosy, Ruff and Curly ran to him at once; and Grizzle got down from his place by the chimney and joined them; while Solo, who had followed the bundle into the room, pulled the window down again.

"What has happened, Daddy?" the two young ones cried.

"Was it a weasel?" said Mrs. Squirrel.

"Humans, I'll be bound," said old Grizzle.

"Ay; they were humans all right," said Solo, while Mr. Squirrel smiled faintly up at Mrs. Squirrel and tried to return the pressure of her little paw.

"Mr. Squirrel here made the great mistake of going

too near that minister's house—*Blink Bonnie*. The Reverend Ebenezer MacDoodle told Willard Wall, the man who does his repairs, that if he saw a squirrel near his house he was to shoot it, and he'd give him a nickel and a half for every squirrel-skin he could get this winter. He says he'll make his wife a fur coat out of 'em."

"Has Daddy been shot?" cried Curly with a gasp of horror.

"Willard Wall got him in the leg with an air-gun," said Solo. "If I'd been there five minutes earlier I'd have sung out to give warning or got Willard Wall himself on the nose with a pine-cone. But I was only just in time to grab your Daddy after he fell out of the big maple at Blink Bonnie. He isn't badly hurt, but I think one of his legs is broken. I've put it in a splint;

and all you'll have to do is to feed him well and keep him warm for a week or two. But I'd choose an inside room where nobody can look through a window. Or —I'll tell you what I'll do. I'll fix this window for you. You'll be safe enough here; for there's no care-taker."

While he was making these remarks, and attending to the window with the broken catch, Mrs. Squirrel, Ruff and Curly were carefully tucking Mr. Squirrel up in a down nest, which Mrs. Squirrel had made with the contents of one of the cushions.

Solo grinned as he looked round at the torn cushion-covers, and the torn book, and the picture on the wall.

"I'd like to see their faces when they come back," he said. "If you take my advice, you'll make for Canada. Medicine Hat's not a bad place, I understand; but you'll be all right here till next May or thereabouts; unless, of course . . ."

He stopped short, as he noticed Ruff and Curly pricking up their ears.

"Unless what?" said Grizzle sharply.

"O, nothing," said Solo. "I'll be on the watch; I'll let you know in good time, if any real trouble should be brewing."

3

SOLO'S TALE OF JACOPONO

SOLO CAME IN to see the Squirrel family almost every evening after that. Very often he brought a little warm milk for Mr. Squirrel. In a week or two, when the convalescent was able to limp about and ready for more solid food, Solo brought them a whole bag of peanuts for their larder.

Occasionally, as the nights grew colder, Solo would light a fire on the big hearth and they would all cluster round the glowing pine-log, and talk or listen to Solo's queer tales of life among the humans.

One night, as the shadows danced on the walls, Ruff asked Solo why he had spoken of "trouble brewing."

"You needn't be afraid of scaring us now," said Curly. "We've got used to the house, and we rather like creepy stories by the firelight. Has it anything to do with weasels? I *am* scared to death of weasels. I saw one, once, creeping after a rabbit. The rabbit ran ten times as fast as the weasel; and then it would try to hide itself in a bush, and the weasel would come creeping, creeping, creeping after it; and the rabbit would come scurrying out of the bush with the weasel close behind it; and, as soon as it had left the weasel a good way behind, it would hide in a bush again, and the weasel would come creeping, creeping, creeping; and the rabbit would come scurrying out of the bush with the weasel close behind it; and every time this happened the weasel would be just a little closer; and then . . ."

She shuddered, and hid her face in her paws.

"It has nothing to do with weasels," said Solo, stroking the back of her head with his big rough hand. "Don't you be afraid of weasels, Curly. Weasels never yet got into a house where a poet lived—not that I ever heard of. Bees, maybe, or bats. But not weasels."

"What *is* a poet?" asked Ruff.

"There was one that used to come to the studio," said Grizzle, "when I lived in the—er—"

"Chimney," said Mrs. Squirrel, helpfully.

"There you go again," said Grizzle, glaring at his daughter, "That is not the right word, as I have frequently remarked. . . ."

"Well," said Mrs. Squirrel, trying to retrieve her mistake, "the what d'you call it, the thingumabob!"

"In the whole course of my only too prolonged life," said Grizzle, "I certainly never called it that! Tut! Tut! It's on the tip of my tongue."

"You mean the round place that was usually full of smoke," said Ruff.

"That's more like it!" said Grizzle with dignity. "The Circles, of course! When I was living in the Circles, a poet used to visit the studio. One day he read a long rigmarole stating that he wanted to be a seagull."

"Lots of 'em say things like that," said Solo. "There was one who wanted to be a skylark. He also wanted to be a cloud, and a wave, and a wind, and a dead leaf, and a lot of other things. But I never heard of one that wanted to be a weasel. I did hear of one who tried to be a turkey. Father Francis, down at the Presbytery, told me about that one day, when I was making him a new hen-house."

"How could anyone *try* to be a turkey," snapped Grizzle. "Either you *are* a turkey, or you're *not* a turkey. You might *want* to be a turkey. But you can't *try* to be one, even if you're a poet."

"This one did," said Solo. "He lived in Italy. His name was Jacopono, which is Italian for Silly James. He did it to annoy his brother, who was going to be married, and was very conceited. This brother had told Jacopono that he must get a new suit of clothes for

the wedding, because it was going to be a very grand
wedding, and Jacopono couldn't possibly come to it
with a great ragged hole in the seat of his trousers.
Well, Jacopono offered to patch it, first of all, with a
piece of red cloth which had once been part of a Car-
dinal's robe. But his brother said that would look ri-
diculous, and he would just as soon invite a turkey to
the wedding. So this Jacopono fills a bucket with a sort
of sticky gum that you get out of the stickiest pine
trees in Italy; and then he goes down to a shed where
they'd been plucking turkeys, and not only turkeys but
peacocks—for over there they used to eat peacocks as
well as turkeys—and the floor was more'n a foot deep
with their feathers. Feathers of all colors, white and
blue and green and, here and there, a red wattle as
well. So what d'you think this Jacopono did? He takes
all his human clothes off; and he smears himself all
over with the sticky gum which he'd brought in the
bucket, and was the stickiest gum that ever oozed out
of the stickiest pine trees in Italy; and then he lays himself down and rolls in the feathers. He rolls in the
little white feathers first, so as to get that downy look.
Then he rolls in the big gray speckled feathers. Then
he rolls his arms in the long wing-feathers; and then he
sits down in the peacock feathers, which were all the
colors of the rainbow. Then he makes himself a kind
of head dress of the red wattles, and walks out into
the glory of the sun. And the first one that beheld him
was a dairymaid, but naturally she didn't know him,

and went off into hysterics, thinking it was a turkey as big as a man. So he struts down to the church where all the guests were assembled; and, just as the priest was saying 'if any of you know any just cause or impediment why these two persons should not be married, speak now, or forever hold your peace,' down the central aisle comes this turkey, as big as a man, strutting and gobbling, and bowing to right and left, and waggling his red wattles, like the most gruesome old gobbler you ever saw, though more colorful than usual, owing to the peacock feathers in his tail. The only thing that wasn't quite right was his feet, which were just naked human. But Jacopono had very flat feet, and skinny drum-sticks and—strange to say—the way he lifted those flat feet up and wriggled his toes, when he strutted up the aisle, made him look more like a turkey-cock than if he'd been a real turkey."

"But what did the bride do? What happened to the wedding?" cried Curly.

"The bride had hysterics, too," said Solo. "She thought it was a judgment on her, for marrying Jacopono's brother when she was promised to a man who kept a poultry farm. So she gave one wild screech, 'Forgive me, Antonio!'—Antonio was the man who kept the poultry farm—and she ran through the church door into the open country, with all the congregation after her, like a lot of little stoats.

"But they couldn't catch her. Jacopono's brother himself couldn't catch her, either. So she married An-

tonio after all; and they say that no man ever had a
wife do better by him. If ever there were words between 'em, Antonio had only to gobble at her, once;
and she'd break off what she was saying, and look at
him with her big dark eyes, and bring him his slippers,
and tell him what a marvelous man he was, and ask
him if he'd like a jug of mulled wine and an omelet
with a strip of bacon for his supper. But he owed it all
to Jacopono being a poet."

"What happened to Jacopono?" said Ruff.

"Well, you see," replied Solo, "nobody knew rightly
who or what that turkey was; and, when his brother
came back from chasing his bride across country, he
went down to Jacopono's cottage and found him just
as usual, lying in the sun outside his door, with the
great ragged hole in his breeches, and just quietly singing another poem he'd been making up out of his own
head. Father Francis told me it went something like
this:

> "What is world's wealth, if we perish despite of it?
> Squirrels and birds know the wrong and the right
>   of it.
> Horses and cows never make such a fuss of it.
> When the hay's ripe, they're content with a truss
>   of it."

There was a sound like the snapping of a dead
branch outside, then the faintest suggestion of a
stealthy footstep, as though someone were prowling
round the cottage.

"Humans," said Grizzle, in a low whisper.

"Ssh," said Solo.

They all held their breath for a moment or two. Then they heard, distinctly enough, the sound of footsteps, going very quietly away through the wood.

"Humans," muttered Grizzle again.

"Ssh," said Solo. "Listen."

And then a very strange thing indeed happened. Away in the distance, exactly like an echo of Jacopono's song, they heard a voice quietly singing. The night was so still that they could hear every word and, though the Squirrels didn't understand them, they seemed to understand the music a little. The song went something like this:

What is this world and the glittering dust in it?
What is its glory, if heart cannot trust in it?
Look at the kings who have kicked up their heels in it;
Rulers and rogues who are turning cart-wheels in it!

Where now is Solomon, once the proud lord of it?
Where now is Cæsar, the red-running sword of it?
All that they wrestled for, wrecked with the rest of it!
Squirrels and birds of the air have the best of it.

It died away, gradually, into the murmur of the pine-woods and the long wash of the sea.

"Who on earth . . . ?" said Ruff.

They all looked at Solo; and to their surprise he said nothing. But his eyes looked darker and deeper than usual. Curly said afterwards that she thought

there were tears in them. But this must have been
imagination, or the smoke of the pine-log. In a minute
or two, Solo said he must be going; and, after carefully
putting the fireguard in front of the glowing embers
on the hearth, he pushed up the window and went out
into the night.

"Goodnight, Solo," they called after him. But, if he
made any reply, it was drowned in the rattle of the
closing window, and the firm thud with which he fixed
the shutters again. It was all very mysterious; and the
squirrels went to sleep that night wondering and wondering who that strange wayfarer could have been; and
whether he had been listening at the door; and how
he came to echo the song of Silly James as he went
through the wood.

4

MYSTERIOUS FOOTSTEPS

THE NEXT DAY the squirrels were out on the roof at sunrise. It was a glorious autumn morning, and the woods all round them were great burning clouds of broken color. The gold of the birch leaves and the blood-red of the maples flamed among the dark pine trees right down to the shore; and the sea below them, breathing gently against the rocks, reflected their colors with the calm of an inland lake.

There was no sight or sound of humans; and, in their happiness, the squirrels neglected one of their precautions, and did not replace the loose shingle which usually closed their private entrance to the cottage. Ruff and Curly took a flying leap directly on to the pine trees, while Mrs. Squirrel and Grandfather

Grizzle gave a paw each to Mr. Squirrel and helped him down by way of the big maple which brushed one corner of the house.

Very soon they were examining the ground near the cottage. Footprints, if they could be found, might tell them something about the mysterious visitor of last night.

Ruff's eyes were sharper than any Mohawk's, and when Grizzle pointed to some tracks that no human eye would have detected among the dry pine-needles, Ruff said at once, "Those are Solo's footprints. I know them because he always goes barefoot, and the big toe on his left foot sticks out more than the other."

Curly, who was a little deeper in the wood, gave a sudden cry.

"What's this? Look, Ruff! It's not made by a bare foot, and it's not like the print of a shoe."

Ruff ran over to examine.

"Curious," he said. "It certainly wasn't made by a bare foot, nor by a shoe. Not an ordinary shoe. But whatever it was, there was a human foot in it. See! Here's the next step; and it's just about the right distance for a tall human."

"And here's the next," cried Curly, running on ahead, "and the next, and the next, and the next. Let's follow them, and see where he goes."

Mr. and Mrs. Squirrel gave a low whistle of alarm but they, too, had caught the excitement, and they followed Ruff and Curly, nudging one another and winking with delight at the smartness of their young. Grizzle strutted after them, shaking his head and mumbling to himself,

"Crazy! Quite crazy! What's the use of going to look for trouble. It'll come soon enough. Let sleeping humans lie, that's what I say. Our skins will be in that Mrs. MacDoodle's fur coat long before the snow comes, I'll be bound."

All the same he was interested, and nothing could have induced him to stay behind. Indeed, when they lost the trail for a time, Mrs. Squirrel gave Mr. Squirrel another little nudge and pointed to Grandfather. Under pretense of a casual search for acorns, he was examining every inch of the ground. Every now and then he would glance rather angrily at Ruff and Curly, to make sure that they were not noticing. They had noticed all right, but they, in turn, were too tactful to show it.

"Derned if I can see any," said Grizzle at last, forgetting his pose for the moment.

"What? No acorns, dear?" said Mrs. Squirrel, who was sometimes so tactful that it sounded like sarcasm, though she didn't mean it that way at all.

Grizzle positively snorted with indignation.

"Acorns! You know very well what I mean. *Footprints!*—You sarcastic little piece of a fur coat! *Footprints!* That's what I mean. Where have they gone to?"

At this moment, a huge porcupine, followed by a small ground-hog, waddled out of the blueberry bushes, stared at them with his little pig-eyes, sniffed contemptuously and lumbered on towards the foot-wide path that rambled down through the wild rose-bushes to the shore. Now Solo had warned them that the huge Porcupine was the leading politician among all the animals in those parts. He was known as the honorable Cornelius. The little ground-hog was, of course, only a clever little fellow who composed his speeches for him, and reminded him when it was time for meals, by going into his burrow and tickling his ear with a straw until he woke and said, "What's the news?" They were

on their way, at this moment, to a private conference, of great importance, with the Skunk.

Grandfather Grizzle was not in the least afraid of the Porcupine. For one thing, he knew that, even at his own advanced age, he could nip up a tree before any porcupine could turn round. So—standing directly in the great leader's path—Grandfather Grizzle made a little bow, and with old-fashioned courtesy (for Grizzle could be almost grimly courteous when he wished) he asked the right honorable Cornelius Porcupine an honest, but perfectly polite, question.

"Excuse me, sir," he said, "but I believe you are usually out all night. We are wondering, my family and I, whether in the course of your—ah—extra-eemly burdensome duties, you happened to see any strange

humans prowling in these woods, between sunset last
night and sunrise this morning?"

The right honorable Cornelius Porcupine stopped
and glared at him. He didn't like being asked questions, because he so seldom knew the answers.

"Have *you* filled up form one hundred and forty-
two B?" he grunted.

"Is that necessary," said Grandfather Grizzle, a little
stunned by so remarkable a retort.

"Ab-so-loot-ly," said the Porcupine.

"Quite—quite," said the little Ground-hog. "Nothing can be done without it. Nothing what-so-ever!"

"Shut up," said the Porcupine. Then, addressing
Grizzle again, he continued:

"On this form, you will have to give all par-ticklers
of yourself. You will have to state the exact number
and length of your whiskers. You must also state
whether they have grown or diminished in number
and size during the last year. If you have no whiskers
you must give full explanations of the fact on form one
hundred and four D. This must be filled out before a
weasel, who will take your Bible oath on it, and make
a record of your finger-prints."

"Will that be all?" said Grizzle.

"By no means," said the Porcupine. "I can't go into
details now. I am on my way to a most important conference with the Skunk."

"Well," said Grandfather Grizzle cautiously. "If a

person wants to know what comes next, what had a person better do?"

"Open his mouth, and shut his eyes, and see what I will give him, sir," said the right honorable Cornelius Porcupine, with warmth. "It's the only patriotic thing to do. Great heavens, Mr. Grizzle, is *this* a time for *questions?* Is *this* a time for thinking? Open your mouth, sir; and shut your eyes, sir; and see what I will give you, sir!"

"Quite—quite! O, heah—heah!" said the little Ground-hog.

"In that case," said Grandfather Grizzle a little proudly, "I don't think I'll trouble you with any questions. I'll just go on quietly looking round myself."

"You can't do that now, sir," said the right honorable Cornelius Porcupine. "The question has been raised, and all the forms must now be filled. The penalty for not filling them, or filling them incorrectly is —er—what is it, Mr. Hog?"

"Smothering for the first offense, sir," said the little Ground-hog, "and skinning for the second."

At this, Grandfather Grizzle burst into a passion of fury, which he had long been trying to suppress. Mr. and Mrs. Squirrel did their best to hold him back, for they knew how difficult it was to deal with a porcupine's thorny defenses.

"You derned little hedge-pig," he cried, "you're worse than the humans. The humans can't help it; but you're deliberately imitating 'em. Smothering and skinning, indeed. You're a disgrace to the woods. And, as for your Skunk, he's nothing more than a Burrow Cat." (Grandfather meant bureaucrat, but Burrow Cat sounded better) "I don't believe he's anything more than a Burrow Cat blowed up with a bicycle pump. If I could get near enough to stick one of your own derned little quills into him, I'd pop his weasel for him. I'd let the gas out of him, double quick, I would. Let me go, Cosy. Don't hold on to me like that. Who's that gripping my tail. Ruff and Curly, if you don't leggo my tail, I'll—"

But they all held on grimly. The right honorable Cornelius Porcupine, elevating all his quills in a crushing and contemptuous silence, waddled away, with two devils' darning-needles flickering in front of him like fighter planes.

"That is the final answer," squeaked the little Ground-hog, putting his fingers to his nose. "There's nothing you can do about it. He has over a thousand quills. And he has followers, and it is their business to follow up them that ain't his followers."

"Followers," said Grandfather Grizzle, "What do you mean by followers?"

"*Weasels*," hissed the little Ground-hog, so viciously that the whole Squirrel family instinctively went a foot or two up the trees that were nearest to them. "That's what I mean by followers—*weasels; and weasels, remember, can climb trees.*"

With that last word he, too, went on his way, with so

obvious an imitation of the right honorable Cornelius Porcupine that Ruff, who was irrepressible, couldn't help a little sneeze of laughter.

"Weasels have pink eyes, haven't they, Grandfather?" said Ruff.

But Curly shuddered, and hid her face again in her soft little paws; and Grandfather Grizzle looked at Ruff so sternly that the jest died on his lips.

"We've been looking for trouble for days past," said Grandfather Grizzle, "and now I believe it's come."

5

FACED BY NINE DANGERS

IT TOOK NEARLY a quarter of an hour to calm
Grandfather Grizzle down, after his quarrel
with what he called the Burrow Cat. The excitement
was not at all good for him at his age. So they made
him sit down in the shade of a huckleberry bush, while
Curly fanned him with a large maple leaf. But he
seemed to be boiling inside, and he continued to ex-

plode from time to time, exactly like a kettle on the stove, when the lid rattles and the steam comes out.

"Of all the impertinence," he cried. "Dye my whiskers blue if I don't go down right now to his—what did he call it—conference, with that there Skunk, and—"

"You know what Skunks are, Grandfather. You'd have to be stripped of every bit of your fur and live out-of-doors till you'd grown a new coat; and winter's coming, remember?"

"I needn't go as near him as all that," the old fellow retorted savagely. "Nobody in my circles ever went nearer to politicians than they could help. But I could climb a tree, couldn't I, and drop rocks on 'em?"

"No rock you could drop would be big enough, Father," said Mrs. Squirrel soothingly. "So you'd better do as you'd be done by. You'd better turn the other cheek, the way Solo says. And, as for that Porcupine, nothing could get through his quills anyway."

Grandfather Grizzle was silent for nearly a minute, thinking about this. Then there came another explosion.

"Red ants!" he exclaimed, so ferociously that Mr. and Mrs. Squirrel leapt nearly a yard away from him, on either side, while Curly tumbled over backwards in front of him.

"Red ants might do it," he went on, in his grimmest buzz-saw voice. "Dye my whiskers green if I don't go down to the anti-hills right now, and see if I can't get a couple of million ants to come along with me. Quills

don't mean nothing to ants; and, anyway, the right
honorable Cornelius Porcupine ain't got no quills on
his stummick."

Before the others had time to reply or to encircle·
him again, the old fellow was off through the wood at
a speed that quite belied his age, and that made it
quite impossible for Mr. Squirrel, with his game leg,
to follow.

"Grandfather! Where are you going?" they called
in chorus. "Don't be rash, Grandfather. Come back!"

But Grizzle disappeared before the words were out
of their mouths. It was not till now that they noticed
the absence of Ruff.

"Where's Ruff?" cried Mrs. Squirrel. "Don't tell me
he's still following up those footprints! We have
enough on our hands for one afternoon."

"No, he's given up the footprints till we have another visit from—whoever it may be," said Curly.

"Then where *has* he gone?" cried Mrs. Squirrel.

"He said he was going to follow the Porcupine, and
bring word back if there was any danger from those
weasels. Oh, and I forgot to tell you. He said he had
just remembered that when we left the cottage this
morning we didn't pull the shingle over the entrance
hole. We were all helping Daddy out at the time, and
Ruff meant to go back and fix it. But he forgot. So he
thought we'd better go back as soon as possible."

Mrs. Squirrel was so agitated this time that she actually said nothing; but she seemed to be trying to walk

in four directions at once. She made three little bouncing steps to the North, stopped; laid her head over her left shoulder, and held out her paws, as though she were saying, "I *ask* you!" Then she made three little bouncing steps to the East; laid her head over her right shoulder, mutely held out her paws in the same questioning manner; and repeated the process to West and South.

Finally, she planted herself in front of Mr. Squirrel and made the same mute gesture.

"Calm yourself, my dear," said Mr. Squirrel.

This was too much.

"Calm myself," cried Mrs. Squirrel, who was usually very placid, but at certain crises could be almost as explosive as Grandfather Grizzle. "Calm myself! Have you, by any chance, drawn up a complete list of the various things we now have to think about?"

"I have not actually drawn up a *list*, my dear; but I think I may say that I have made a mental note of them."

"Then let us go through it," said Mrs. Squirrel.

"I am quite agreeable, my dear," said Mr. Squirrel, who always became more mild and more precise in his language in exact proportion to the excitement of his spouse. "I am quite agreeable, my dear."

Picking up a pine-cone she threw it at him as hard as she could. It hit him right on the tip of his nose, and bounced off so hard that she caught it in her right paw and prepared to throw it again.

"I think you misunderstood me, my love," said Mr. Squirrel ruefully feeling the tip of his nose. "When I said I was quite agreeable, I was not suggesting for a moment that I was a pleasant character. I meant that I entirely agreed with you that we should go through the list."

"Very well then, my ser-weet," said Mrs. Squirrel. "First of all, there's your game leg. We'll call that exhibit A. You won't deny you broke that, will you?"

"Shall we say that Willard Wall and I broke it between us, my love. I think that would be fair."

"Very well, then, take that!" retorted Mrs. Squirrel, letting fly at him with the pine-cone and hitting him on the tip of the nose for the second time.

"Dear me, Cosy," said Mr. Squirrel, "that *did* rather hurt, you know. But—" he added, "you're a remarkably good shot."

"Secondly," continued Mrs. Squirrel, fiercely, "there's that prowling human, who left the footprints. How do we know it wasn't the Reverend Ebenezer MacDoodle?"

"We are in complete accord there, my love. We know nothing whatever; but I am inclined to think it was something more mysterious than the Reverend Ebenezer MacDoodle."

"Then, thirdly," Mrs. Squirrel went on, "there's that fur coat he promised to Mrs. MacDoodle. Where's that to come from?"

"Our skins, undoubtedly, my dear. But that *does*

depend—to a *certain* extent—on whether he can get them."

"Exactly," Mrs. Squirrel replied. "So I hope your fifth mental note is Willard Wall, who has been offered large sums of money to secure them—a nickel and a half, I believe, for each skin. Then, sixthly, there's Grandfather Grizzle gone completely potty. Where is he now? On the rampage in the woods trying to raise an army of ants to attack the right honorable Cornelius Porcupine! Seventhly, there's Ruff, disappearing off the face of the earth—"

"Surely, my dear, not *quite* off the face of the earth —so far as we *know*—" Mr. Squirrel tried to suggest; but Mrs. Squirrel was not to be appeased.

"Disappearing heaven knows where," she insisted, "on a trail which will lead him into some loathsome den of porcupinal horror where he will probably breathe his last in the clutches of a Skunk. And if that's not off the face of the earth, I should like to know what is. Eighthly, we have been threatened with following up by weasels; and ninthly, but by no means last, the door to our comfortable little house, where we were to be so happy for the winter, has been left wide open, so that weasels may crawl in while we are away, and lie in wait to suck our blood when we return."

"I admit," said Mr. Squirrel, in his most soothing tones, "I admit that the prospect you paint is *dismal* in the extreme, but—"

"Good heavens," cried Mrs. Squirrel, "don't talk to me like that—"

"Like what, my love?"

"Why—as if I were the wife of a bullfrog!" squeaked the little darling in a perfect fury.

"I will try to do better, my sweet. Your phrases are really quite electrifying. The only question in my mind is whether the sombre picture is, in every detail, quite true. You see, my dear Cosy, there would hardly be time yet for the following up by weasels; and, if we hurry back, at once, I have no doubt we shall be able to make everything quite safe, and be ready to welcome Grandfather Grizzle and Ruff when they return."

"I doubt whether I shall ever see either of them again," said Mrs. Squirrel sharply. But she evidently agreed that they had better get back home as soon as possible. She bestowed what looked like the smallest of all possible kisses on Mr. Squirrel's injured and unexpecting nose; and—with Curly close behind them —they went off together, as quickly as Mr. Squirrel's game leg would allow, in the direction of Blueberry Cottage.

6

RUFF'S ADVENTURE

change

IN THE MEANTIME, Ruff had plunged into an adventure so extraordinary that he forgot all about the mysterious footprints. He was able to follow the Porcupine and the little Ground-hog with the greatest ease, of course, and without being noticed; for, while they lumbered slowly through the bushes Ruff went nimbly overhead through the maples and pines and silver birches. He kept to the maples, for the most part, since the blood-red of their leaves blotted out all the color of his own coat and bushy tail. But he needn't have troubled himself about this; for

42

the Porcupine and Ground-hog lurched along with their noses to the ground, and never once looked up at the tree-tops or the sky.

The sunlit tree-world seemed a much pleasanter place this morning than the more shadowy world below; and Ruff was so agile that he had plenty of time to enjoy it and exchange chirrups with a friend or two among the birds. Sometimes he would leap on to the swaying young leader of a tall fir and ride it, while he waited for the two creatures below to make their way across a piece of difficult ground. It was not wise, the older squirrels always said, to leap on to these young and tender leaders; but Ruff was young, too, and if the bough broke he knew that he could instantly alight on another. He was riding on the topmost bough of a spruce—he liked the pungent smell of the spruces better than any other of the thousand scents of the forest—and the topmost bough was still wet with dew. There were sprinkles of it on his coat and on his face. He put out the tiniest of tongues to taste it and found it most refreshing. On the topmost spires of some of the larger pine trees he could see a large herring-gull staring out to sea. A human might have said that it looked as though the pine trees were bearing great white magnolia blossoms. But Ruff was a squirrel; so —to him—it looked only as though herring-gulls were roosting on pine trees; and the pine trees were dark; and the herring-gulls were white, freckled with brown;

"Surely this is very irregular!"

and the sea, at which they were staring, was as blue as the sky.

But Ruff was enjoying it all so much that, although he was right about the herring-gulls, he was almost as much in the moon for half a minute as a human could have been; and in that half minute a startling thing happened.

A beautiful bird, rather larger than a thrush, fluttered onto the bough below him, and remarked, '*Tsee! Tsee! Tsee!*' Ruff knew him well. It was the cedar waxwing, and, unfortunately Ruff thought that the remark, *Tsee! Tsee!* was only the waxwing's usual way of saying 'goodmorning'; or perhaps an invitation to admire its soft brown wings, and the beautiful shining red patches on them which humans have compared with sealing-wax. But the '*tsee! tsee!*' was hardly uttered when the waxwing suddenly shrunk, as though afraid that something were going to fall on it. Ruff instinctively looked up at the sky; and there he saw a very strange thing indeed. It was undoubtedly a bird; but, unlike most birds, it seemed to be frozen stiff and still in the air directly over his head. Ruff did not know whether this was for the benefit of the waxwing or himself. Before he had time to think about it, something did fall. It was exactly as if a great wind had rolled itself up into a solid ball, and dropped out of the sky with a terrific thump into the spruce tree. Ruff went head over heels into space, vaguely aware of claws and feathers and what he described afterwards to Solo as "a sort of bluggy smell"; and the next moment with his bushy tail acting as a parachute he landed on all fours immediately in front of the great Porcupine. Above him, in the sky, he caught one glimpse of the duck-hawk, wheeling away with something in his claws—something that had wing-feathers marked with red, like sealing-wax. But he was too startled to be sure. He sat up slowly, erecting his own tail; and stared at the right honorable Cornelius Porcupine, who stood not more than six inches away, with all his quills bristling and a most vicious look in his wicked little eyes.

"What does this mean, Mr. Hog? Surely this is very irregular," the great creature snorted to his attendant.

"O, quite—quite—most—*most* irregular," squeaked the little Ground-hog, who feared that he was going to be blamed for the incident. "But you see, sir,"—he added flatteringly—"It is very difficult to discourage the natural public interest in your coming conference with the Skunk. This curious intruder may be a newspaper reporter. I understand they often arrive in these odd ways, tumbling out of trees and things."

"Reporter! With a tail like that," the Porcupine answered contemptuously. "Unless I'm mistaken, it's one of those Squirrel brats." Then, turning to Ruff, he said in a fiercer voice, "Ain't I right?"

Ruff was too frightened to reply except by lifting his bushy tail.

"You see," exclaimed the honorable Cornelius, "he

confesses. Now tell me, and be careful that you conceal nothing," he went on to Ruff, "what were you doing in that tree?"

Ruff still could not speak. But he picked up a pine-cone, cracked it open, took out one of the nuts, and showed it to the Porcupine, as if to explain that he had been looking for food. This was partly true; because Ruff was always looking for food.

"Nuts, eh?" said the Porcupine. "And laying 'em up for the winter, I'll be bound. Isn't there a ruling against that, Mr. Hog?"

"O, decidedly, most decidedly," squeaked the little Ground-hog.

"And the penalty?" asked the honorable Cornelius.

"Well, sir, we usually follow 'em up with weasels, first; and when the weasels have finished with 'em, there's not much left to do."

"Hah!" said the Porcupine, "Well—I have no doubt that these Squirrels have been laying up nuts for the winter. We must take steps, immediate steps." With this, he actually advanced a step towards the almost petrified Ruff, and made so gruesome a rattling with his quills that Ruff could hardly keep his tail erect or his teeth from chattering.

"Where is your family living?" demanded the Porcupine.

Ruff made a wiggling motion with his tail, so that it pointed in all directions around the forest.

"A tail is not the most satisfactory means of communication," said the Porcupine. "Have *you* any idea where these thieving creatures have been laying up their nuts for the winter, Mr. Hog?"

"No, sir," squeaked the Ground-hog. "But I can easily find out. I rather suspect one of those deserted cottages. The Skunk may be able to tell us about that. He has been nosing around most of the back-doors and garbage cans lately."

"We must find out, at once," said the Porcupine. "They must be followed up with weasels. Weasels may not be able to catch 'em awake; but they can catch 'em asleep. It's the following up, by night and day, that does it. Bring him along, Mr. Hog. Grab him by the tail and bring him along."

But ground-hogs, even in those alarming conditions, are not as nimble as squirrels; and that last sentence aroused Ruff from his trance of terror. He was half-way up a silver birch before the Porcupine had finished his sentence. From the silver birch, he leapt into a pine, from the pine into an ash tree, and from the ash tree into the gorgeous colors of a great spreading maple, in which it was quite impossible to see him, or distinguish him from one of the more shadowy leaves. But Ruff could see his enemies, and watch every movement.

Many young squirrels after so disturbing an encounter might have hurried home to warn the family about those weasels; but Ruff was pluckier than most, and he had great confidence in his nimbleness. He felt it would be more satisfactory if he did a little following up himself, and found out exactly what the Porcupine and his supporters were going to do. He was more careful after the shock he had received; and he now kept to the farther side of the boughs through which he ran, only thrusting out his head occasionally to make sure that he was on the track of his enemies.

In a few minutes they came to a white wooden cottage in an open clearing, overlooking the sea. It made Ruff a little nervous again when he recognized the cottage as Blink Bonnie, the summer abode of the Reverend Ebenezer MacDoodle, who had left those grim instructions about squirrels with his caretaker, Willard Wall. It was where Mr. Squirrel himself had been shot only a short time ago; and Ruff was glad to find a hole in a tree where a chickadee had nested last spring. It was a delightful observation post. It commanded the very spot, near the verandah of the cottage, where the great meeting was to take place between the Porcupine and the Skunk. All that Ruff had to do was to sit down comfortably on the abandoned nest within the hole and look through a little opening as though he were in a tiny box at a theatre.

The great Porcupine and his companion had no suspicion that they were being watched. They probably thought Ruff had been so frightened that he was halfway home by this time; and they waddled up to the verandah as though they owned the place. And a very beautiful place it was. Two large Norwegian pine trees, one on either side of the small grassy ledge in front of the cottage, framed a glorious view of a long reach of sea running endlessly into the distance, between chains of pine-darkened islands. In the long grass, the late bees and butterflies still hovered over tall autumnal wildflowers, and below their feathery whisper the sea breathed like a child asleep. The windows of the cottage were shuttered for the winter; and the only sign of humans was the little red buoy of one of Willard Wall's lobster traps, rising and falling gently with the lapping blue water below. A human might have compared it to a poppy asleep in a wide rippling meadow of violets; but Ruff was a squirrel; and to him it looked exactly like the red buoy of Willard Wall's lobster trap.

The little Ground-hog made a scratching sound on the lowest of the sun-baked wooden steps that led up to the verandah. Apparently, it was under this wooden verandah that the Skunk had taken up his residence for the autumn; for almost immediately after this signal the Skunk appeared, resplendent in his black and white fur coat. He stood looking at the great Porcupine, about five yards away; and the honorable Cornelius stood looking at the Skunk; as though they both doubted the wisdom of going nearer.

"Before we begin," said the Skunk, in a curiously thin voice, "it is understood, I suppose, that quills are barred."

"Certainly," replied the Porcupine. "But I should

like to be assured that, on your side, there will be no—er—" here he gave a rather loud sniff—"positively no—er—what shall I call it?"

"You needn't call it anything," said the Skunk," the question of—er"—here he gave a rather louder sniff himself—"can hardly arise between friends."

"I agree, in principle," returned the Porcupine shrewdly, "but how do I know you have no Indian reservations?"

"Indian reservations? What do you mean?" said the Skunk in a peevish voice.

"Crossing your fingers when you make me a promise," said the Porcupine. "How can I assure my friends that you've not done that?"

"Why, that's quite simple," said the Skunk, "I can promise you that I won't cross my fingers, can't I?"

"Do you think that's all right, Mr. Hog?" said the Porcupine. "Do you think that will satisfy our side?"

"I think they will want him to promise that he won't cross his fingers when he promises that he won't cross his fingers," said the little Ground-hog, shrewdly. "Then everyone will see how honest and straightforward we all are."

"Thank you, Mr. Hog," said the Porcupine, "Now let us get this matter straight. We both of us promise that we will not secretly cross our fingers—er—er—"

"When we promise that we will not secretly cross our fingers," continued the Skunk, helping him out. "We agree to promise that we will not cross our fingers on any occasion when either of us promises the other that—er—" Here he, too, seemed to be a little puzzled, but the little Ground-hog came to the rescue.

"When either of the high contracting parties promises the other that he will not secretly cross his fingers," he concluded. "That should be quite enough, as between honest folks, anywhere."

"Very well," said the Porcupine, "We'll leave it at that."

It seemed to Ruff that it might have gone on for ever, like the oldest of all riddles:—*Which came first, the hen or the egg?* But the Porcupine and Skunk appeared to be satisfied for the moment; and, as they were what Mr. Hog called the "high contracting parties," it was their own affair. Besides, the most honorable Cornelius Porcupine was in a hurry about something. Ruff noticed that quite a number of ground-hogs had assembled behind him.

"*Is the Chief Weasel here?*" the great Porcupine asked, in a voice that vibrated through every separate hair in Ruff's bushy tail; and, immediately, a long yellowy snake-like creature came streaking out of a hole near the steps, and stood near to the Skunk, blinking its red-rimmed eyes at the Porcupine.

"*Is the Butcher-bird here?*" said the Porcupine, in an even nastier voice; and, instantly, there alighted on the verandah steps, just behind the Skunk, a large black and white bird with a fieldmouse in his claws. Ruff knew him. It was the Shrike, commonly called the

Butcher-bird, owing to his unpleasant habit of killing more than he needed to eat and hanging up his prey on thorn-bushes. The black and white of his feathers matched the Skunk's fur coat beautifully; but he was a nasty fellow for all that; and the offhand way in which he picked up the mouse and impaled it on a rusty nail at the edge of the verandah made Ruff's blood run cold.

"Before we discuss anything else," said the Porcupine, "there is a charge against a number of Squirrels, who must be taught a lesson. The Butcher-bird handles a mouse very neatly. I suppose he could deal with a young Squirrel or two."

The Shrike gave a harsh laugh, as much as to say, "dozens, if necessary."

"Very well," the Porcupine answered, "The Butcher-bird and the Chief Weasel may begin the following up at once, if my right honorable friend, the Skunk, agrees."

"What exactly is the charge against the Squirrels?" said the Skunk. "Not that it really matters. We can always make up a good charge. But I like to know."

"*Laying up nuts for the winter,* is the main charge," replied the Porcupine, "It's quite a popular charge among my people. It sounds good to charge 'em with that."

"Think of 'em looking ahead like that! Laying up nuts for their brats in the winter! Do you suppose they have been laying up anything else—more interesting than nuts?"

"I'll be bound they have," said the Porcupine. "All kinds of eatables. They've a whole room full of apples; and not only apples, but all the things *you* like to eat."

This of course was untrue, but the Porcupine wanted the Skunk's help, and, being a great politician, as we have already seen, he didn't care very much what he said, if only he got what he wanted.

"Lots of 'em?" inquired the Skunk, pretending not to be greatly interested.

"Garbage cans full," replied the Porcupine.

"Then what are the Chief Weasel and the Butcher-bird waiting for? Why don't they follow 'em up, right away?" said the Skunk, with a sudden briskness, as though he had made up his mind what to do.

"We are not *quite* sure, at present, where this hoard has been hidden," said the Porcupine.

"I—can—tell—'em—*that*," drawled the Skunk, slowly, while a very sly sideways look came into his eyes. "In fact, I think I'd better go with 'em myself and show 'em the way."

"One minute," said the Porcupine, who had noticed the sly look. "It's understood I suppose that the hoard will be distributed among us *all* equally?"

"Depends on what you mean *all*," said the Skunk.

"He means *us*, of course," squeaked all the ground-hogs behind the honorable Cornelius. "He means *us!*" And they were so delighted with this explanation that they rolled themselves up into round prickly balls at the thought of it.

The Porcupine shifted uneasily from one foot to the other; for this was not at all what he meant by equal shares for all; but he could not disappoint his followers at this early stage. So, being a very great politician indeed, he thought it best to make a speech that *might* mean what the ground-hogs thought, but *really* meant what the Porcupine thought.

"*Ahem!*" he said, clearing his throat. "In principle, of course, I agree entirely. When I said *all*, I meant that *all* would eventually benefit; but *all*, of course, includes *some*. Nobody can deny that. Now those who are responsible for the welfare of the woods, naturally come first."

At this all the little ground-hogs looked at one another uneasily.

"However," the Porcupine continued, "what we obtain from the hoards of those greedy little creatures who presume to lay up nuts for their horrid little brats to eat in the winter, when their elders can no longer look after them, will be quite enough for the comfort of us responsible persons whom they have the impudence to call Burrow Cats."

There was a pause, after this bewildering burst of eloquence. It was broken by the Skunk.

"Do they call *you* a Burrow Cat?" he asked, in a voice that sounded like icicles in vinegar.

"They regard *Me* as the arch Burrow Cat," replied the Porcupine proudly.

"I see," said the Skunk, enviously. "But I don't suppose they call *Me* a Burrow Cat, do they?"

"They do indeed," said the Porcupine. "They call you the piebald Burrow Cat."

"Piebald!" exclaimed the Skunk, suspiciously. "Does that mean I get only a half-share?"

"Not at all," said the Porcupine. "I'm afraid it's an insulting allusion to the very striking effect of your magnificent fur coat."

"I—see," drawled the Skunk, venomously. "Well. I think I'll be moving along, with the Chief Weasel and the Butcher-bird. I'll show 'em the way to the—"

"One minute!" said the Porcupine again, standing directly in the path of his dear friend, the Skunk, "Wouldn't it be more satisfactory if you told us all beforehand exactly where it is, and exactly what you are going to do?"

"I—think—not," replied the Skunk. "You move too slowly, and you arrive too late; so, in any case, we should be there first. Besides, I entirely disapprove of giving unnecessary information to the public, or indeed to anybody."

"But surely—to *Me,* your friend—at a time like this!"

The Porcupine stood facing the Skunk, as he spoke; and, without realizing it, he allowed his quills to bristle slightly.

"You remember our agreement—quills to be

barred," drawled the Skunk, in a hideously sneering voice.

"Naturally," said the Porcupine, hastily lowering his quills.

"Very well," drawled the Skunk, in an even more hideously sneering voice.

The Porcupine sniffed at the air uneasily, and remarked in an agitated sort of way:

"You remember, of course, your own promise that you would not secretly cross your fingers when you promised that you—"

"Met a fiddlesticks," said the Skunk, lowering his head abruptly and pattering curiously with his fore-paws.

The Chief Weasel made a nasty hissing sound.

"Look out!" squeaked the little Ground-hog, while all the smaller ground-hogs bustled off into the bushes, squeaking, "Look out! Quick! Run!"

Then, something very queer happened, too quickly for the warning to be of any use to the Arch Burrow Cat. Ruff couldn't quite see what it was; but the right honorable Cornelius Porcupine clapped a paw to his right eye and exclaimed hastily, "Good heaven, Mr. Hog, *where* is my gas-mask?"

At the same moment, although he was much farther away than the Porcupine, Ruff himself became aware of the most gruesome smell he had ever smelt. It made him feel very sick at the stomach; for he had a sensitive little nose, and he loved all the sweet-scented things in the forest. He loved the scent of bayberry leaves, and honeysuckle, and pine-cones. He could distinguish in the dark between all the trees of the wood, simply by their fragrances. He knew the refreshing smell of the good brown earth after rain; and the comfortable smell of the blue woodsmoke when Solo lit his pine-log fire in the golden autumn evenings.

But this was something new. He wondered if it was what the humans, according to Solo, sometimes called "frightfulness." It was a kind of earthquake among smells. Ruff didn't know much about human words; but he felt that the Skunk had certainly earned his name. It was a wonderful name. It said everything in a word of one syllable. He felt that no word in all this world could describe a Skunk better than just that one little syllable—*Skunk*.

The Skunk himself, of course, had not stayed to enjoy the sensation. He had gone off at a great pace through the woods with the Chief Weasel and the Butcher-bird, in the direction of Blueberry Cottage. Ruff was on the point of being horribly sick, when he was distracted from his own feelings by the spectacle of the Porcupine below. If it is possible to be stunned by a smell, that's exactly what seemed to have happened to the Porcupine. He was waddling backwards, in a weak-kneed waggling sort of way, waving his front paws before his nose, and exclaiming faintly, "Mr. Hog, where *are* you? I believe I have been gassed."

The right honorable Cornelius Porcupine was not a sensitive creature, but he had been standing very close to the Skunk, and he had apparently received a large part of the smell in his right eye.

This naturally made it difficult for him to steer straight when he was waddling backwards; and, after he had crashed heavily into a thorn-bush he made a half-circle round the clearing; and, finally, to Ruff's astonishment, backed blindly into the very hole which formed the entrance to the Skunk's winter-quarters, under the wooden verandah of Blink Bonnie. His front paws were still waving before his nose as he disappeared backwards; and, a moment later, Ruff heard him spluttering and bumping and thumping about in the Skunk's house, as though he were furiously trying to find the way out again.

It looked as though this would take him a long time. It is much easier to go through a hole by accident than to find the same hole again when you are going backwards in the dark.

The crashes and the bangings were succeeded by a strange scrattling sound, which filled Ruff with curiosity. He was on the ground in an instant, and drew cautiously near to see what was happening. It was extremely interesting. The Porcupine had backed into the Skunk's house with his quills down; but, in his blind fury he had allowed them to bristle again; and whenever by some happy accident he found the hole and tried to back out, his quills stuck in the wooden framework and held him there kicking and shoving like a mad ferryboat that has been blown into the wrong dock by a squall. In fact, when Ruff peered at him, it really looked as if the right honorable Cornelius Porcupine were permanently fixed there.

"What an opportunity," Ruff thought, "for Grandfather Grizzle's ants to get under his quills." Then, at the thought of Grandfather Grizzle, he suddenly remembered that Blueberry Cottage itself was in great danger; and that the Chief Weasel and the Butcher-Bird, under the direction of the Skunk himself were already on their way to it.

They had a start of several minutes; but Ruff, thinking he could still get there first and warn the family, went off through the trees so quickly that you could hardly tell whether he was leaping or flying.

Possibly that was why, for the second time that day, something fell on him from the sky; something that crashed down on him in mid-leap, like a great wind that had rolled itself up into a ball of feathers with a hard core of bone. But this time, instead of hurling Ruff into space, it caught him with two fierce claws (fortunately, by his bushy tail) and wheeled off and away with him.

Up, up, up, till he wondered dizzily whether he was being taken to one of the crisp white clouds that were sailing through the upper sky. Far below him he saw, first, the green heads of the trees growing curiously small; then, to his amazement, he was high over a creeping blue reach of the sea; and then he saw one of the pine-darkened islands beyond it growing mysteriously larger. It seemed to be swooping up to meet him with all its red rocks and trees and soft little curving beaches. He could smell the seaweed. He could hear the wash of the sea among the rocks, and the clamor of a hundred herring-gulls that rose like a cloud of spray from a breaking wave. Then something else unexpected happened—to his kidnapper. Two great ospreys who had apparently been acting as sentries for the island had been disturbed by the approach of the duck-hawk. Ruff could see them rising, one on either side, above his kidnapper. Then he saw them swooping murderously down, one from the east, and one from the west. The duck-hawk swerved violently to avoid them, plunged almost to the level of the tree-tops; and, in yet another violent swerve upwards to avoid a whole squadron of angry herring-gulls, he dropped Ruff into the bushy top of a pine tree, and wheeled back to the mainland. Ruff was very dizzy, and quite unhurt. But he was in a real predicament now. He was separated from the mainland, and Blueberry Cottage, by at least a mile of salt water. He could actually see Blueberry Cottage and Blink Bonnie, among the trees on the opposite coast. But he was marooned as completely as Robinson Crusoe. There was all that danger to his family, and no way of warning them. The beautiful little island on which he had been dropped was uninhabited by humans; it was a little Paradise for birds and bees; and, in other circumstances, it might have been a Paradise for Squirrels. Indeed, the Indians who used to hunt and fish there called it Pooduck Island; and Pooduck means the place where the world ends.

7

THE MISSING SHINGLE

Mr. and Mrs. Squirrel, and Curly, had arrived at Blueberry Cottage later than they expected; for Mr. Squirrel's leg was still not very strong; and they made several halts on the way. But everything seemed just as quiet and peaceful as usual. There was only one thing that puzzled them. Their private entrance, which had been so carelessly left open, was a good deal larger than when they last used it. This morning, only one of the neat shingles near the chimney had been loose. Now there were two.

Mrs. Squirrel felt very uneasy about this.

62

"I hope those weasels haven't got into the house already," she said, sniffing suspiciously at the opening.

"Weasels," said Mr. Squirrel sagely, "would certainly not need to make the door larger. Moreover, if one shingle could come loose chew-it-ously—"

"Chew-it-ously," cried Curly, startled by the vivid suggestions of that first syllable, *"What* do you mean by *that*, Daddy?"

"Chew-it-ously, my dear, is a more select word for *by chance,"* replied Mr. Squirrel, who—as we have already seen—was rather proud of his choice of words. "Time and Chance have a way of chewing things to pieces."

"Well!" exclaimed Mrs. Squirrel, who was growing angry at being entangled in conversation at so dangerous a crisis. "Well! I don't wonder that the weasels are after us. Look at that door! Twice as big as it was this morning! Three times as big! Four times as big! And, as *everyone* would say, *wide open.* As wide open as your mouth at this very moment. So how do *we* know what has got into that cottage? Will you please give me your *ordinary* ideas about that; and, if you use a single select word about it, I shall scurr-eam!"

Mr. Squirrel was really just as nervous as Mrs. Squirrel about that open door. He quite understood his wife's excitement; but he thought it best to appear as unruffled as possible.

Mr. Squirrel, therefore, poked his head through the door with the caution of a Mohawk peeping into the wigwam of a Sioux. After a very careful scrutiny of the room within, he decided to enter. Mrs. Squirrel and Curly followed; and, this time, they closed the door behind them, by drawing the two loose shingles into place. It was concealment rather than door-closing; for the slightest push would have dislodged the shingles. But this might be an advantage, if dangerous visitors had really got into the cottage; for the Squirrels might have to leave in a hurry.

Everything, however, seemed to be exactly as they had left it. The last down-cushion, which Mrs. Squirrel had been so busily ripping apart to make a bed for Ruff was still exactly as she had left it. Not a feather, so far as she could see, had been stirred. Their larder was untouched; and Mr. Squirrel pointed out that the little bag of acorns which Grandfather Grizzle kept in his chimney-corner had not been disturbed.

"I remember Grandfather Grizzle saying he had exactly ten acorns left, and wondering whether Ruff and Curly would be getting him a fresh supply soon," he remarked.

There was really an ample supply in the cottage for the whole family. They had been laying it up for weeks. But it was a fad of Grandfather Grizzle's to keep a small private bag so that he could chew whenever he felt like it.

Mr. Squirrel emptied out the acorns and began to count them.

"There are ten, and two over," he announced triumphantly. "That settles it, I think. It would be fantastic to suppose that anyone has broken into the cottage with criminal intentions, when Grandfather Grizzle has not only the original ten in his bag, but two over."

"Grandfather Grizzle can only count up to ten," said Mrs. Squirrel.

"True, my dear," replied Mr. Squirrel. "But he would at least have known that there were two over. Having counted up to ten, I think that—without any *great* mental effort—he might, so to speak, begin again, and count the remaining *two*. I have looked very carefully at our own supply of nuts; and I am positive that they have not been touched. I took note, only this morning, of the exact position of the nuts on the top of the pile; and I can assure you, positively, that not one of them has been displaced by so much as a hair's breadth."

It was Curly who brought this argument to an abrupt end.

"Weasels don't eat nuts," she said.

The truth was that all the Squirrels were bundles of what Mrs. Squirrel called "instink"; and, unconsciously, they felt that they were surrounded by new dangers. Mr. Squirrel, like many humans, had been whistling to keep his courage up. Curly's remark flattened him out completely.

"I *wonder* . . ." he murmured to himself, looking anxiously at the darker end of the room.

"My in-stinks . . ." began Mrs. Squirrel.

"I feel sure there is *something* in the house," said Curly.

"I am *positive*," said Mrs. Squirrel.

"I really *do* begin to wonder," said Mr. Squirrel, in a voice just as low and creepy as it had been brisk and confident a minute ago.

There was a curious sound at the dark end of the room, from somewhere above the gallery.

The Squirrels huddled together in the big chimney-corner, staring in the direction of the sound. In the dim light they could see nothing there but the glimmer of the silver-birch-work, and the black crossbeam eight feet above it.

Then, suddenly, they *did* see something—so frightening that they could only creep closer together and stare. About a foot and a half above the black beam two glowing moons of fierce yellow fire had opened in the darkness, and seemed to be glaring straight at them. It was an unwinking and motionless glare; but it could mean only one thing—*eyes*. They were much larger than any weasel's eyes. They were too far above the beam to belong to a wild cat. There was only one thing of which the Squirrels were sure—they were *eyes*.

8

GRANDFATHER GRIZZLE'S
REVENGE

ON THAT SAME AFTERNOON, Solo was lying among the ferns, not far from Blink Bonnie, looking over at the islands. He would have liked to go and see his friends at Blueberry Cottage again this evening; but he had promised Father Francis that he would bring him a bucketful of clams from Pooduck Island. There was nothing the old padre liked better for his evening meal than a clam chowder. Solo planned, therefore, to go to Pooduck Island in his canoe, very soon. It was not quite time yet. He could dig for clams only at low tide, and the clear water had hardly ebbed from the red rocks below. So he lay in the ferns, looking now at the pine-darkened islands in the distance; now at the broadening patch of wet pebbles and seaweed from which the tide was quietly withdrawing.

It was very pleasant lying there in the long grass, between the wood and the sea. It made him feel drowsy, so drowsy that, when the queer sounds began, he wondered whether he had fallen asleep and was dreaming. Then he really felt he *must* be dreaming; for this is what he thought he saw and heard.

First of all, from the direction of Blink Bonnie, there came a series of resounding thumps, as though a muffled drum were trying to beat itself black and blue in a fit of very bad temper. Then, from the wood on the other side, only a few yards from where he was lying, there came a faint and very curious creeping sound. It was almost like the breath of a very low wind creeping through the pines; but it came in regular beats, like the sound of innumerable insect feet marching in time. In fact, it was a marching sound, but instead of going *tramp—tramp—tramp,* it went *creep— creep—creep.*

Then, only a yard or two from his eyes, where he lay staring at it, through the fringes of fern and Queen Anne's lace, the most amazing procession went by. At the head of it, with his bushy tail up, came Grandfather Grizzle, strutting along on his hind-legs in the

most conceited way and twirling a great Michaelmas
daisy in his hand, like a drum-major. Behind him
marched an apparently endless army of large red ants,
goose-stepping in perfect time and much more effec-
tively than humans could do it, for ants have six legs.

They were so intent on their purpose, whatever it
might be, that they took no notice of Solo, even when
he sat up, rubbing his eyes and trying to count them.
He knew that the ant power of the woods was im-
mense; but he had no idea, till he saw them marching
past, what a great people it was. He wouldn't have
believed there were so many ants in the world. On
and on they went, endlessly; and the spit and polish of
their shining dark red armour was as admirable as the
precision with which they threw out their legs. At last,
as the tail of the column actually disappeared, with a
small contingent of centipedes undulating behind it in
the most formidable way, Solo gave his eyes another
rub and decided that he must have been dreaming.
Possibly he had, if there is any truth in the remark of
one of his poet-friends, that the whole world is made
of dream-stuff. But it wasn't an ordinary dream.

Grandfather Grizzle, in fact, had been having a
grand time. He had really meant what he said to Mr.
and Mrs. Squirrel about finding a way to get under the
quills of the Porcupine; and, being happily unaware of
the startling adventures of the rest of the family during
his absence, he had not been distracted from his plan.
He had found a large colony of ants in a soft-mounded

hillock not far away; and, though he was unable to talk their language, he could convey amazing things in dumb show. In fact, Grizzle's dumb show was almost as vivid as Indian picture-writing; only, of course, it was done in the air; so that no record was left of it. This afternoon he had excelled himself. First, he held up an apple—a windfall from a neighboring orchard—and pointed to the holes made in it by ants. This had a personal appeal which naturally gripped the attention of his audience. Then he split the apple open and showed them three startled ants who, supposing themselves to be completely shut off and secure from the outside world, had been only too comfortably nibbling at the core. This appeared to amuse the other ants very much, if ant amusement can be measured by the contortions of their slim waists, and the wild waving of their antennæ; and, indeed, nothing appeals more to ants, or to humans, than pleasant discoveries of this kind.

Grandfather Grizzle then made a graphic circular gesture with his forepaws, indicating that he knew of a much bigger and better apple, or something equally good to nibble, out there in the woods. This was received by the whole ant audience, now several hundred strong, with twistings and prancings, and pincer-like movements of the mandibles, which certainly looked like extreme enthusiasm.

A deep hush followed. Grandfather Grizzle, pointing to the fallen elm, under whose wrinkled crust some of them would have been contented to pass the rest of their lives, gave the most contemptuous sniff that had ever come from his nostrils. He was no orator but he could tell them, with a sniff, that they had been hood-winked, if not defrauded, when they were led to be-lieve that this was a fit life for ants. He indicated, by rubbing his stomach and rolling his eyes, that he knew of pleasures far finer than burrowing under the bark of a rotten tree. The way he broke off a piece of that bark, smelt it, and tossed it haughtily away, would have convinced a wood-worm.

He paused for a moment, to make them feel that something tremendous was coming. Then, with the most realistic twiddlings of his dainty little fingers, he suggested to them the infinitely more exquisite de-lights of *wriggling under the woody quills of a living porcupine*. He showed them, by the most graphic motions, amid wild whistlings and scritches of laugh-ter, how utterly impossible it was for a porcupine to scratch his own back; or, indeed, for anyone else to scratch it for him, *unless one could get under his quills*. He showed them how, even if the porcupine rolled, he could never dislodge an invader who really did get under his quills. He showed them how the quills would actually protect such an invader from injury. In fact, he painted an ant's Paradise, with all the fun of the fair as well; and, in less than no time, he had a whole army of ants marching behind him. He led them, first, to the clearing where he had last seen the right honorable Cornelius Porcupine, and had been so browbeaten. They soon picked up the heavy creature's trail; and a few minutes later they were marching through the pines, where Solo saw them, on the way to Blink Bonnie.

Solo went on rubbing his eyes for almost a minute after the tail of the column had disappeared. Indeed, the disappearance itself made him think it must have been a dream. He recalled a line that Father Francis used to quote, from a queer play about Midsummer Night,

"Following darkness like a dream."

But his reasoning was not quite true. A great many things disappear that are not dreams; and the hush that had come over the wood was deceptive.

Suddenly, from the direction of Blink Bonnie where, during the passage of the ant army through the wood, the strange thumpings had ceased, there came a new and stranger sound. The muffled drum seemed to have gone quite mad, and was not only beating itself, but squawking like a gigantic goose. Solo leapt to his feet and went swiftly, on tiptoe, towards Blink Bonnie. He peered through the pines, at the edge of the clearing, in which the cottage stood, and there—dream or no dream—he saw a sight such as the Reverend Ebenezer had never seen in all the summers he had spent there.

Grandfather Grizzle was standing alone, in the middle of the clearing, with his head cocked on one side, intently watching the hole under the wooden verandah. Inside this hollow structure, and under the wooden steps in front of it, a miniature hurricane seemed to be taking place, accompanied by loud squawks that sounded like very bad swearing in an unknown tongue. Whenever there came a louder crash than usual Grandfather Grizzle executed a joyous little step-dance and twirled the great Michaelmas daisy over his head. He was so intent on the hubbub under the verandah that it wasn't until Solo chuckled that Grizzle looked up and saw him.

"What's happening?" said Solo.

"The right honorable Cornelius Porcupine," said Grizzle. "He's in there. We've got him! Under the quills! Red ants!"

There was a terrific crash as the right honorable Cornelius backed for the fourteenth time into the hole with all his bristles up, and stuck there, scrattling and puffing like a panicking grampus, while Grandfather Grizzle broke into a perfect Highland fling of delight.

"Ay; but you'd better be careful. You see, he's losing his quills," said Solo. "And he'd lose 'em quicker if he'd got wits enough not to go stern foremost. Why is he doing that?"

"He's been making no end of a song about it," chirped Grizzle. "Seems he met a Skunk here, before we arrived. Seems he got it in the right eye. If you get it in the eye as well as in the nose, you can't get rid of it for weeks and weeks. It gets into all your pipes and passages. Isn't it heavenly?"

"Look out," exclaimed Solo. The Porcupine who had again gone forward, with a resounding thump, under the verandah, had been accidentally bumped into the right course, and appeared to be careering round his prison at a speed which could only mean that he was now going head foremost. Suddenly, out he came, liked a scared wild pig. Grandfather Grizzle was halfway up a tree already; but he needn't have troubled himself. The right honorable Cornelius had urgent affairs elsewhere, and could be heard crashing and rolling through the undergrowth a hundred yards away.

"He won't get rid of 'em unless he wallows in the creek for a couple of hours," said Solo, "and then they'll probably get into his ears. Where are you off to now?"

"Going to tell the family all about it, at Blueberry Cottage," said Grandfather Grizzle.

"Give 'em my love," said Solo. "I'll be coming round to see you all tomorrow night. I'm off to Pooduck Island now, in my canoe. Going to dig clams for Father Francis."

"Campin' there tonight?"

"Most likely. I've got my sleepin' bag with me. See you tomorrow."

And so they parted, each to his own adventure; Grizzle to a scene very unexpected at Blueberry Cottage; Solo to the island which the Indians had named Pooduck; and *Pooduck,* as we should remember once more, means the place where the world ends.

9

NIGHT ON POODUCK ISLAND

IN THE LITTLE COVE below Blink Bonnie, Solo
waded out with his canoe. He was always careful not to scrape her on the barnacled stones and sharp
mussel shells of the beach; so he was knee-deep in the
water before he got into her. Then he stripped off his
jersey and shirt and dipped his paddle for Pooduck
Island. He had spent most of the summer in his
blue dungaree shorts, and his skin was browned to
the color of a red Indian. Very like an Indian he felt,
too, as he dipped his paddle and made for what had
been one of the Red Man's happy islands—Pooduck,
the place where the world ends.

He liked to visit Pooduck. He could be quite alone
there with his wild creatures. In summer he would

sometimes sleep there for three or four nights at a time, living on the fish he caught by day, and the wild strawberries that grew in the meadowy patches between the clumps of pine. There was a delicious water-spring on the island, and he used to build his fire between the rocks on the beach, where the spring ran down to the sea. No rich man's banquet ever tasted so well as the flounders that Solo fried at that fire, or the potatoes that he took over with him and baked and ate in their skins, or the dessert of wild strawberries or blueberries that followed.

Pooduck Island was not more than six hundred yards long and three hundred wide. It was big enough for Solo to lose himself in; yet small enough for him to feel that it was his own island. It had miniature beaches; miniature forests; miniature meadows; and a miniature trickling stream, by which wild blue irises grew at the right time of the year. But when the sea-mists drew round it, and cut off all sight of the mainland, it seemed to grow curiously big. It became a world by itself then, and Solo was its king. At such times, it had a strange way, too, of remaining sunlit, while all but a narrow ring of sea around it was lost in the mist.

In the early summer, its wild little meadows were perhaps the loveliest part of it. There was one where the herring-gulls nested, and you had to walk carefully to avoid treading on the big brown-spotted eggs, usually three of them at a time in the circle of flattened grass which was all the nest that the herring-gulls ever made. There would be dozens of these nests in July; and a little later the young birds would be running through the bracken, like downy little ducks; while the older birds wheeled overhead, screaming the most awful accusations at any intruder. But not at Solo. They knew Solo now; and, if he picked up a young bird and stroked its wings, it would lie as quiet as if it were his little brother, and turn its head and look up at him in the friendliest way; while the older birds, after the first startled exclamation, would settle on the tops of the tall dark pine trees and watch with a kind of proud approval, sometimes pretending more indifference than they really felt; yet, on the whole, rather pleased that their offspring had enjoyed this unique experience.

But it was more than this that made it so magical a place for Solo. Neither he nor anyone else could have put it into words; but it was the way in which a certain rounded gray rock stood up in the meadow with a cluster of poppies at its side. It was the keen scents of the tiny vetches, and the wild thyme and a hundred other sweet breaths. It was the low sea-wind blowing across the red and white clover when he lay down in it and sucked the honey out of their little trumpets. It was the way in which the tall feathery grass and the white ox-eye daisies stood up between him and the foam-feathered blue of the sea. It was the gaps and ragged arches between the dark pines through which he saw that dazzling blue again over ferny hollows. It was the little wild raspberries that stained his bare feet. It was the bees and the small blue butterflies with their freckled underwings, that seemed so soft and tender to be out there on an uninhabited island. It was the hardier and fiercer things in the background —the black cormorants on the red rocks, and the ospreys on the tallest pines. It was the sleek seals that hauled themselves out of the water and lay basking in the sun, with such strangely human movements of their heads, as they turned to look at him. It was the way in which the sea-gulls would carry a clam or a mussel twenty feet up into the air and drop it on to a rock to break the shell, just as if they wanted to show Solo how closely akin they all were. It was all these, and many other mysterious things which, for Solo, always made it seem so good for him to be there.

Near the spring, where Solo carried his canoe up the beach, there was a white shelving bank made entirely of cracked and chalky fragments of old clam shells. It was so old that the chalk had begun to settle down into a miniature white cliff, and the grass and the wild-flowers had long been growing on its top. It was the place where the Indians used to gather for their clam-bakes; and, several times, when a part of the bank had crumbled away after rain, Solo had found a relic of the old days—an arrow-head, or a fragment of an Indian cooking-pot. Father Francis had been greatly interested in these; and Solo thought that, when he had got all the clams he wanted, he would explore the bank with his clam-rake, and see if he could find anything else to interest the old padre.

He was lucky with his clams this afternoon. Between the mussel-beds, which he avoided because they cut his feet, the tide had left dark patches of a soft quaggy sand, pitted with round holes into which you could have put your finger. If he trod within a foot of them they squirted salt water at him as if they were deliberately trying to show him where to dig for the finest and biggest clams in Maine. In a very short time he had filled his bucket, and sat down to rest for a moment by the canoe.

It was about half an hour before sunset now, and the mile of sea between him and the mainland was already sleeking itself into that evening smoothness which he loved. The pine-woods along the coast looked darker and clearer; yet the air was diamond bright; but the water seemed to be growing more and more softly opalescent. Halfway to the mainland, a huge gray-blue heron went solemnly winging home to the reeds of the Penobscot River; and across the West there was already a faint wash of rosy color.

Solo sat by his canoe, drinking it all in for a few minutes; then he picked up his clam-rake and climbed to the top of the crumbling white bank. At the other side of the meadow, a herring-gull was dragging itself through the grass in an odd way, with one wing outstretched. Solo ran up to it and found that it had been badly wounded. He took the bird in his arms and soothed it, trying to examine the injury more closely. It was a curiously shaped gash—almost triangular—in the breast. The herring-gull had been savagely attacked by an osprey and it seemed impossible that it could live many hours. Solo could not bear to think of it lingering on in pain. He thought it might be kinder to kill it—quickly. But he had never killed things. He wondered how he should do it. He touched the smooth little head, and looked at a rough stone. He could crush it, instantly with that. Yet—it didn't seem the right way, on Pooduck Island. The herring-gull lay quietly in the fold of his bare arm and against his bare breast. Once it turned its head and looked up at him, curiously. . . . He couldn't kill it, after that. There was nothing that Solo could do about it, except to make it a little bed of soft grass among the sheltering ferns. It settled down there, quietly, as if it were going to sleep. Solo knelt by it, watching it for some time; then, with a last gentle touch, and a whispered goodnight, he rose to his feet and went a little way up a miniature woodland ride of tall bracken through a clump of fragrant red cedars. He did this because he thought he saw a light shining at the end of it. Suddenly, he stood quite still, knee-deep in the bracken and caught his breath in a gasp of sheer wonder.

A few yards in front of him, there was one of those gaps or ragged arches in the wood, through which you saw the sea again, just as if you were looking through some wild cathedral window, in which all the colored glass had been re-placed by the shining and living colors of the sea beyond. But this time it was more beautiful than it had ever looked before, even to Solo; for the lower part of that wild window, arched by its dark cedar boughs, was a glowing mass of tall purple loosestrife, with the opaline sea shining *through* the blossom as well as above it; while, away in the distance, he saw a three-masted full-rigged schooner of the old days, growing slowly brighter as she crept along the dark background of the coast to take the first colors of the sunset on her crowded sails.

He stood there, for nearly five minutes, watching her. It was like looking through an eye of his beloved Island, and seeing things more clearly and beautifully than he could see them elsewhere. Then, slowly, the opalescence of the sea changed into a light mist, rising in wisps and wreaths and at last veiling the magical picture completely. It was like the mist that, once or twice, had dimmed the eyes of the wounded herring-gull, he thought. Then he turned and went back to the spring where he intended to camp. It was the same there, too. Filmy curtains of mist had hidden both the mainland and the islands, leaving only a narrow ring of sea visible around Pooduck, which had once more become a world in itself. Yet, most curiously, Pooduck Island and its narrow ring of sea were still bright with the last of the sun.

Solo turned to the white bank of chalky shell-stuff,

and began to dig in it. He hoped very much that he might find another Indian relic or two for Father Francis; and he had hardly scratched the surface when a gleam of red caught his eye. He dug it out with his hands to avoid damaging it with his clam-hoe, and gave a cry of pleasure to find that it was a finely cut Indian pipe of red stone—the kind that they smoked at their peace councils. Solo thought that Father Francis might like to substitute it for the long church-wardens or hot little corncobs that he usually smoked in the winter evenings. He would have to give it a new stem, but that would be easy. The head of the pipe had an Indian face on it, beautifully carved. Solo knew where that stone had been quarried. There was only one place in North America—the sacred mountain of the Red Man—where it was to be found. The pipe could probably be sold to a collector for a large sum; but Solo wanted it for Father Francis, and never thought of its money value. It may have been for this very reason that so many strange things now began to happen to him.

It had been rapidly growing darker; and, as he stood admiring the pipe, polishing the bowl against his dungaree shorts, he had his back to the sea; so that it was not until a strange hand touched him on the bare arm that he knew he was not alone. He turned swiftly and saw, facing him in the half light, a tall dark and very dignified figure, wearing an Indian headdress of richly colored eagle feathers which could only belong to a Sagamore of the highest rank.

"Solo has found it!" he said; and his voice was as deep and musical as the sound of a low sea-wind through a red cedar.

It could only be the red stone pipe that he meant; and Solo held it up to him, smiling,

"Yours?"

The Sagamore folded his fringed blanket around him with the pride of a Roman senator, and shook his head, slowly and gravely.

"Not mine," he said. "But it may not be good to have found it."

"Whose?" whispered Solo; for he was so awestruck by this strange apparition that he could hardly speak.

"It came from the sacred mountain," said the Sagamore. "It belonged to Glooskap."

"Glooskap, the mighty?"

"Glooskap, the mighty. I knew him, from afar. He was my friend, in time of great trouble."

"But that was more than a hundred years ago," Solo whispered again.

"When the mists are round it," said the Sagamore, "there is no time on Pooduck Island."

Solo looked at the pipe again. He saw now that it was of no common workmanship, and there was a mysterious beauty in the carven face that made him think of things that live forever.

"Do you wish to take it back to him?" he said.

"Solo has found it," the Sagamore replied. "And now it belongs to Solo. I came only to warn him."

"To warn me—of what?"

"Good fortune," said the Sagamore.

"Good fortune," cried Solo. "I thought everyone wished for that."

"That is why I came to warn you," replied the Sagamore. "Let Solo fill this pipe with the herbs that the Indians used, and light it on Pooduck. Then, while the smoke is rising, he may wish anything that his heart desires, and it will be given to him. Could any good fortune be greater than that?"

"There are many things I could wish," said Solo. "I could make good use of this pipe."

"A hundred years ago," said the Sagamore, "there was a fool of the Mohawks who thought the same. He was a very small man. They called him the Chipmunk; and he could hide where no full-grown Indian could hide. But his tribe laughed at him, and he was too small to bear laughter. One day he crept up a rift in the Mountain, where no other Red Man could go; and he came upon the wigwam of Glooskap, at the hour when Glooskap slept among his own clouds. The red stone pipe had slipped from his hand; and the fool seized it, and stole away with it. He crept down the rift in the steep face of the Mountain; and, when he came to the forest below and was only a little way from the tents of his tribe, he stopped in the middle of a clearing and looked at the pipe he had stolen. And the bowl of the pipe was still warm, like the egg of an eagle that has been newly taken from the nest; for it

was filled with the medicine leaf that Glooskap himself
had been smoking, and the fire was only asleep in it.
So the fool of the Mohawks, whom they called the
Chipmunk, set the pipe to his lips, and drew, and
breathed out the blue smoke, as he stood there in the
clearing, with only the pine trees watching him. And,
while the smoke was rising up to mix with Glooskap's
own clouds in the sky, he uttered the wish that had so
long been gnawing at his heart; for he was a very small
man. 'Make me,' he said, 'taller than the tallest of the
Mohawks, so that none will ever mock at me again.'

"And, as the words left his lips with the smoke, he
stretched up his arms and stood like one praying; but,
when the prayer was ended, his arms were still up-
stretched, and his feet were rooted in the ground, so
that he could not move them. And a strange prickling
numbness flowed through him, as though the sap were
flowing upward through his body from the earth where
he was rooted; and, slowly, he grew upwards; and the
skin of his body grew dark and rough like the bark of
a pine tree; and his arms grew slowly out like the
boughs of a pine tree; and his fingers bristled like the
young shoots of a pine tree; and his face was like the
yellow patch where a bough has been lopped off by the
axe; till the young branches drooped over it from above
and hid it from sight. Then, in the place where he had
been standing, there was only a pine tree. It was taller
than any of the Mohawks. It was taller than any of the
pine trees in that forest. But it was only a pine tree."

"Must it always be so, with all wishes?" said Solo.

The Sagamore was silent for a moment. Then he gave one of the wisest answers in the world.

"I do not know."

"I would like to try it," said Solo. "Not for myself. If we wish for ourselves, I can understand that there may be a great price to pay. But—if we wish for others—"

"Perhaps, even then, we or another must pay the price," said the Sagamore. "Perhaps that is—the great secret."

Solo turned this over in his mind for nearly a minute. There seemed to be something very deep in it. Then he replied:

"I would still like to try it, with just one very small and harmless wish. Up yonder, in the meadow, I found a wounded herring-gull. It will not die for several days, and it will be in pain. There can be no harm in wishing to take away that pain. I thought, first, of killing it; but I couldn't. It didn't seem the right way, on Pooduck Island. Besides . . . it looked at me."

"I know that look," said the Sagamore.

"Let us try the pipe of Glooskap," said Solo.

The great Chief bent his head to examine the pipe more closely. Then, from under the folds of his blanket-robe he drew a pipe of his own. He detached the long stem, and found that it fitted perfectly into Glooskap's pipe. Solo went to the canoe, and got his lighter out of the camping-kit. Then they went up the white crumbling bank together and moved swiftly across the little meadow to the place where the wounded gull was lying. There was blood in the nest that Solo had made for it, and its breast was dabbled with red. It looked up at them, and made no attempt to struggle when Solo gently lifted it and showed the gash in its breast, under the right wing. It was a curious triangular wound.

"Let us try," said Solo, as he laid it down.

The Indian had filled the bowl of the pipe from his own wallet, and held out his hand for the lighter.

"Squando will kindle it for his friend," he said.

Solo started as he heard that name, once so terrible along all that coast from the Penobscot to Quebec. But, for the moment, he had to think of the herring-gull. He remained kneeling by the nest, while the Indian, standing on the other side, set the little flame to the bowl, drew at the stem, breathed a long spiral wreath of smoke towards the sky, and handed the pipe back to Solo, as if the important part still remained to be done. Solo remembered afterwards that, as the Sagamore breathed the smoke from his lips, his eyes had been half-closed, and he had that strange rapt look on his grim face which, like the mysterious beauty of the carved face on the pipe itself, made one think of the things that live forever. But Solo did not think of it now.

Still kneeling by the nest, he put the pipe to his own mouth, drew deeply and breathed a thin fragrant cloud of smoke towards the sky, wishing with all his heart; while the Indian stood, like a statue of bronze, watching him.

"Look," whispered Solo.

The herring-gull's eyes had been dim and half-closed. They were growing round and bright. It stretched its brown-spotted wings as though it were lazily waking out of a long sleep. As the wings lifted, the red stain was visible on its breast, but the ugly gash no longer showed, and the smooth breast feathers were all in place. A moment later, with a contented little cry, it rose into the air, wheeled twice overhead, as though to thank them, and disappeared over the cedars into the thinning mist.

Solo rose to his feet.

"It came true," he said breathlessly, "and no harm has been done."

The Indian stood, looking at him, silently and a little sternly. He did not reply or move, except for one second when he twitched the folds of his blanket more closely around his breast. The name that he had used of himself—Squando—was one of terrible memory. He had a grim and, in some ways, a terrible face. Solo looked at him with a new wonder and said, "Squando does not answer. Is it because he thinks the price is yet to be paid?"

"Everything is bought with a price," said the Sagamore; and when he said that, he looked like a king.

"Squando spoke of a time of great trouble," said Solo

softly, "when Glooskap was a great friend to him. I have thought of Squando as one who killed without mercy, never as one who knew compassion or—grief."

"Before the Paleface came in the great sailing ships," replied the Sagamore, "and began to give us evil for good, there was much happiness among my people. We did not need to die to find the Happy Hunting Grounds. Sometimes a death would break our hearts; but we did not break our word. It is true that Squando killed without mercy. It is true that his people went back to the beast with the white man's fire-water. But there *was* a time, before the killing began, when Squando knew love, as well as grief. There was a time when Squando had a little son, playing on the hemlock floor of his tent or sleeping on a blanket before the campfire; and in those days Squando was not unmerciful; for the little one played in his heart as well as by the door of his tent; and there were good men, like your Father Francis, who came to us from France and would have led us into the ways of peace."

"But, one day, when the little son of Squando was playing on the banks of the Kennebec River, two soldiers of the Palefaces came by. They had heard that the children of the Indians could swim in mid-stream from the hour of birth; and they wished to see if it were true; for they were lovers of knowledge. This was their tale. So they flung the child into the waters of the Kennebec; and stood on the bank laughing, while it fought for its life. . . .

"And, after it had sunk and was drowned, they came, still laughing, to the mother, and offered her a gift of fire-water, and three pieces of silver, instead of her little son."

"Laughter . . . and gifts . . ." whispered Solo, as if he had seen something too terrible for belief.

"Worse than gifts . . . worse than laughter," said Squando. "For they were hypocrites. They laughed in their hearts and tried to hide it in their faces; and she *saw*—she *saw* the mockery of grief on their mouths and the grin in their eyes. It was what the Palefaces called the reserve of the well-taught; but they did not trouble to hide it overmuch. She heard them laugh aloud, in the woods, when they had left her.

"It was then that Squando went mad. He wanted to kill, without mercy. And then—he found the pipe of Glooskap under a pine-tree, and brought it to Pooduck Island, thinking he might use it to . . . to revenge his . . . to do justice on. . . ."

The Sagamore wrestled with his own thoughts for a moment, then continued.

"It might have given Squando all he wished in war, and the home of his fathers might have been rid of the Paleface forever. But he never used it."

"Why?" whispered Solo.

"Glooskap was a great friend to me. He spoke to me in the night. A man may work or fight for his wish with his own hands. He may ask for it in prayer; but it is not good for him to tell the gods what they shall do. It may be that the price would have been all that remained to Squando—and that he would have lost the mother of his little son. She was very dear to him."

"The white men all say they have nobler thoughts than that," replied Solo; but it sounded as though he would prefer not to believe it. "In all their wars, great or small, the white men have said they would give all those little things away to defeat their enemies. Were those little things dearer to Squando than his country?"

"Perhaps that is why the great ones, with their fire-water, have defeated us, here, for a little while," said the Sagamore. "This world will not last forever. Who knows what price the white man will have to pay for his wish? Squando was never great or wise in the way of the white men; and before he and his people became the brutes they made us, a little hand in his was a better thing than any war can win. It is better, even now."

He was silent again, for a long time. It seemed that the waves washing softly round Pooduck grew stiller and stiller, till Solo could hear the beating of his own heart. All at once he noticed that Squando was breathing as if in pain.

"You are hurt," he cried.

Squando looked at him quietly for a moment. "The price was a very little one tonight," he said. "But it may be well for Solo to see that it has been paid."

As he spoke, he drew aside the folds of his blanket and showed a ragged and bleeding wound in his side.

It was a curiously shaped triangular wound, exactly like that in the breast of the herring-gull. It might have been made by the beak of some savage bird.

Solo started to his feet, with a cry of compassion; but, almost instantly, the Sagamore folded his blanket around his breast again, and said:

"It is nothing. It will soon heal—if Solo will fling the Medicine Pipe of Glooskap into the sea. Squando will give him a far better gift for Father Francis."

Solo handed the stem back to Squando. Then, without a word, he ran down to the beach and hurled the red stone pipe, with its beautiful carved face, as far as he could, into the sea.

When he returned, Squando was waiting for him at the top of the white crumbling bank. Something very beautiful was shining in his brown hands. He held it out to Solo.

"For Father Francis," he said.

It appeared to be a long Indian necklace of wampum. The seashells, of which it was composed, were small in size, but of the most exquisite form and color that Solo had seen in his life.

"It belonged to the mother of Squando's little son," said the Sagamore. "She wore it when she was dying. Father Francis will understand."

Solo took it in both his hands, and made his own queer little sounds of delight over its loveliness. The night was clear now. The mists had melted away from sea and sky as quickly as they had risen; and the moon, shining over the red cedars and silvering the foam along the shore, brought out a hundred iridescent gleams in the wampum necklace as he drew it shell by shell through his trembling fingers. At the end of it he touched something that told him it was what Father Francis called a rosary. He looked up to thank the Sagamore; and—there was nobody. There were only the dark cedars in the background, made all the darker by the almost dazzling whiteness of the crumbling bank in front.

"Squando!" he called; but there was no reply.

He was alone, once more, on Pooduck Island, and *Pooduck,* as we have seen, means the place where the world ends.

Ruff, not knowing that Solo was there, had been drowsing in a tree-top at the other end of the island. He woke up at that call, and listened. But it did not come again; and he thought it must have been one of those voices that come to you in your sleep, when you are troubled. For Ruff, too, had a heavy little heart. There were no Squirrels on Pooduck Island. Somebody he knew would be missing him at Blueberry Cottage; and he did not see how he was ever going to get back to it. He thought of many strange plans while he was drowsing. Sometimes, in winter, he had heard that the water froze quite hard and firm between the island and the mainland. But years might pass before that happened again. Occasionally, a moose had been seen swimming across the sea-reach, with

little more than his great antlers branching out above
the water, like boughs from an oak-stump. Ruff wondered whether he might perch on one of those boughs
and be ferried over by the moose. It was a brave
little plan; but unfortunately there was no moose at
present on Pooduck Island. So, although he did not
think about it quite as humans might have done, he
just felt as if his tongue were very dry. It couldn't
be that; because he had moisted it in the dew, many
times, before he went to his tree-top. He felt, too, as
if his heart were being pinned in a wire-trap; and
that couldn't be true either because traps can't get
inside you—not if you're a Squirrel. For the present,
therefore, there was nothing to be done but to go to
sleep, if he could. He was very tired; and sleep, being
kind to squirrels, came quickly.

Solo had gone down to the spring, near his canoe,
where he meant to sleep. But it was long before his
eyelids closed. The humming *soo-soo-soo* of the pine-
woods; the low *ssh-ssh-s* of the sweet-grass which the
Indians may still use for their basketwork; and the
lapping of the salt water over which, in lonely places,
the Indians may still creep out in their birch-canoes
to gather it; all these were saying the same thing to
Solo as they had said in the old days, hundreds of years
ago, before the French and English wars. Perhaps
they had said it since the beginning of the world.

At last, as his eyelids closed, all the different sounds
began to keep time with his own breathing; and he

knew that he was listening to a song. He couldn't tell
whether it was outside him or inside him. It was the
song of someone who might have been very happy,
once; but had been made unhappy by the humans. It
was the song of the passerby who had left those mysterious footprints near Blueberry Cottage, and had
disappeared, singing, through the woods. He was pass-
ing by, once more; and the music was the same, but
the words were different. They sounded like this:

Squirrel corn, squirrel corn, dig for the sweet of it!
Gold cannot buy it, but squirrels can eat of it!
Mother and chickaree, up now, and run with it
Back to your tribe, if you'd play in the sun with it.

Run thro' the sweet-grass, and back to the tent with it!
Light was their laugh on the wind—and they went
    with it.
Torn away, torn away, arrow and quiver,
Into what darkness, O wild rushing river?

Wide is the world. Was there never a nook for them?
Where the world ends, let the Sagamore look for
    them!
Lost in the night of his heart, and still nigh to him,
Where the world ends, in the dark, they still cry to
    him:

Squirrel corn, squirrel corn, racing the chickarees
Down to the blossom-patch, under the hickories,
Run thro' the sweet-grass, or sleep in a nest of it,
Mother and little brown son have the best of it!

10

RAW SKUNK

WHEN GRANDFATHER GRIZZLE reached the clearing where Blueberry Cottage stood, he took his usual precautions. He had a lot of exciting and glorious news to tell the family; but he sat on a bough of the big maple which overhung the roof, and looked round him very carefully before going farther.

The first thing he noticed was the Skunk, nosing round the back-door. Grandfather Grizzle chuckled at this, for there was no garbage now that the humans had gone away.

The second thing he noticed was the Butcher-bird on the ridge of the roof. There was nothing, except the way in which his black and white plumage matched the Skunk's fur coat, to suggest that they were work-

96

ing together; but Grizzle felt uneasy. He was glad to
see that the Squirrels' private entrance-hole was closed,
or rather concealed. He knew, of course, that a touch
would discover it; but he didn't suppose the Butcher-
bird really knew anything about the Squirrel fam'',
within, or that he meant mischief to the ___

The next thing he notice', however, chilled his
blood. It was the Chief Weasel's flat snake-like head,
a ver___ ss triangle of pale yellow, with glittering
little green eyes, peering over the ridge of the roof.
The long slim pliable neck switched to and fro as
though it worked on a swivel; then the Chief Weasel
decided to come over to the hither side of the roof.
He ran over it in circles, sniffing at the shingles for
the scent of his prey. All at once he became wildly
excited. He ran straight to the entrance by the chimney; and thrust his sharp nose between the two loose
shingles, which instantly slipped apart. The Chief
Weasel drew back and looked at them as though to
say—'that's odd.' Then, to Grandfather Grizzle's horror, he went through the hole like a long streak of
yellow-brown water slithering smoothly into a drain-
pipe.

The Butcher-bird uttered a nasty squawk of approval and, fluttering down from the roof-ridge, poked
his own head through the hole; while the Skunk disclosed his own interest by taking up a position in
front of the cottage from which he could watch the
Butcher-bird. The latter, however, after a brief ejacu-

lation or two, apparently addressed to the Skunk, suddenly decided to follow the Chief Weasel into the cottage. The Skunk thereupon climbed heavily up to the top of a wood-pile, from which he could get a better view of the roof and await events.

An extraordinary silence followed. Grandfather Grizzle could hear a fir-cone dropping in the wood twenty yards away. He was unaware of the savage eyes which—for the last half hour—had been holding the Squirrel family hypnotized with fear in their chimney-corner. He had ears quick enough to detect the slightest flurry inside the cottage. But the silence was so intense that he thought the whole Squirrel family must still be out in the woods. If so, it would be best for him to wait where he was, and warn them, when they arrived, not to enter.

All at once the silence was broken and events began to happen very quickly indeed. First there were two terrified little shrieks, which Grandfather Grizzle felt sure had come from Mrs. Squirrel and Curly.

It was followed by a wild mixture of sounds. This wild mixture included a huge soft thump, like the thump of an umbrella when a high wind suddenly blows it inside out; and a nasty thin hissing sound, like objections from a lot of little snakes. There was a still nastier snarl, suggesting that somebody's teeth were being bared to the gums; and there was a particularly horrid growl, which might have come from a goblin in the act of strangling his wife. There was, at the same time, a heavy *wallop—wallop—wallop,* as though an enormous bird in a furious temper were trying to dust the room with his own wings. There was a terrific crash of broken crockery; and a harsh blood-curdling scream, which certainly did not come from any of the Squirrel family. It sounded very like the whistle of a train that had gone crazy and was plunging into a pitch-black tunnel full of mice. But it was an orchestra, not a mere succession of sounds; and they were all happening together. To Grizzle's amazement, in the middle of it all, he was almost sure he heard a faint shout of *'hurrah'* from Mr. Squirrel. The harsh blood-curdling scream, however, outlasted all the rest. It shot up towards the hole in the roof; and—to Grizzle's intense interest—not only shot *up,* but shot *out,* with a frantic look in its eyes. It was the Butcher-bird. He had lost half the feathers in his tail; and, if ever a Butcher-bird was saying, *'Get out of my way! I'm in a hurry!'* that Butcher-Bird was saying it now.

The next thing that happened was that the yellow-ish brown head of a huge horned owl came up through the hole, with three of the Butcher-bird's missing feathers in his hooked black beak. His round savage eyes, flaming like yellow lamps in the gathering dusk, stared after the fugitive exactly as if he were saying, *'Let me catch you trying to poach again!'* Then, so soundlessly and swiftly that it looked like magic, Baron Bubo—for that was the name of the Horned Owl—

was out of the hole and standing majestically on the roof-ridge. He had dropped the feathers out of his grim beak; but in his claws he had brought something else, even more interesting. He laid it on the roof as though it were no more important than a dead mouse. But it was the limp body of the Chief Weasel.

Grizzle could well see why the Chief Weasel seemed unimportant to Bubo, the Horned Owl, who stood there so grandly, with one claw sinking into the slim

body of his prey. Bubo might be as wicked as his almost Satanic horns would suggest, but there was no doubt of his magnificence. He had the largest and most amazing eyes of all the winged folk in the forest; and the warrior beak of a Norman king between them. The black stripes across the tawny yellow of his breast and the white patch at his throat were almost lost in the dusk; but one felt that he could have talked with a tiger, as one king to another.

The Skunk, who had been watching events from the top of the woodpile, was not at all anxious for kingly conversations; for, if there is one thing which the Horned Owl likes for his chief meal it is a certain fat and savory food called skunk-liver. It was at this precise moment, therefore, that Skunk decided to retreat. But, as he occupied his high commanding place on the top of the woodpile, the retreat would depend a good deal on what the enemy did to *him* before he got down. Indeed, at his very first movement, the Skunk was aware that two great yellow searchlights were glaring at him from the roof-ridge. He felt as if his legs were turning into soft-boiled macaroni.

His first step, therefore, was to stand quite still, in the hope that he might be mistaken for a bunch of flowers that somebody had left by accident on a woodpile. Nobody but a human, however, has ever mistaken a Skunk for a bunch of flowers; and the unwinking yellow lamps that were fixed upon him did not belong to a human. They belonged to the Horned Owl.

The Skunk, however, being a politician, realized this; and, being also the slowest-witted of all the creatures in the woods, he tried silently to explain the situation to himself, just as he might have to explain it later to his followers. *My plan of standing still*—he thought to himself—*was well considered. Everything so far has gone according to plan. It is true that the Butcher-bird has lost his tail; but let us remember the far more important fact that he still has his wings. It is true that the Chief Weasel is dead. But so—unless I am greatly mistaken—is Queen Anne. We are faced now with the fact that Owls are not humans; and circumstances alter cases.* (This struck him as a very valuable thought indeed for his followers, so he though it all over again.) *Circumstances alter cases. Very well. The sands are running out. The acid test is at hand. I am in the front line, and must be prepared for sacrifice. But of two things I have no doubt whatever*—he found this so comforting that he actually whispered it very softly to himself—*I have no doubt whatever. I must be prepared to explore new avenues, and take a further step in the public interest.*

Unhappily, just as he had moved his right foot one inch forward, a badly balanced log on the woodpile slipped under him and gave the signal for the Horned Owl to swoop.

And a wonderful swoop it was! Bubo struck exactly the right spot, so that no further question of being skunked could arise.

Grandfather Grizzle danced and shouted deliriously on his blood-red maple bough; but there was so glorious a rattling and scattering of the silvery woodpile that one couldn't be sure of what he was saying. It was undoubtedly something enthusiastic about the way in which the Skunk was tumbled off the woodpile, while the Horned Owl was searching for his most appetizing titbits. He was tumbled, first into a patch of wild autumn flowers which are sometimes called white rosemarie, but on this occasion certainly deserved their country name of *Farewell Summer*. The Skunk was then thoroughly dusted over with the golden pollen of black mustard, and rolled into a further patch of blue chicory blossom. To complete the joyful picture, a long vine of late-flowering honeysuckle (the garden kind) had gra-chew-it-ously (as Grizzle would say) wreathed itself about the Skunk's fat tummy, exactly as if he were being dressed for the table of a Tudor king. It is not surprising that Grizzle found the spectacle inspiring, and even dramatic. What he shouted was apparently in rhythm, for his dance kept time with it. It *sounded* like this:

Some likes chickun-pot, and some likes goose.
Some chews venison, and some chaws moose;
But *I* know a hero as wily as a 'possum;
And *he—likes—raw—Skunk,* sassed with meadow blossom.

O, nuts are good to nibble where the Squirrels keep house.

Bears are all for honeycomb, and minks eat mouse;
But *up* with your fiddles! Let 'em *plunk—plunk—
  plunk!*
Here's to the hero who can *eat—raw—Skunk!*

A maid may bottle blueberries and eat 'em with a
  spoon.
An Injun pick a turkey, or a woodchuck, or a coon;
But *I* will declare it, to my last death-ruckle,
He—likes—raw—Skunk, trimmed with honeysuckle.

so

A bow for the Johnny who was called Jack Sprat,
A scrape for his missus who could finish off the fat,
A fig for the elephant who fiddles with his trunk;
But a *Whoop* for the hero who can *eat—raw—Skunk.*

The gorgeous feast by the woodpile began immediately; and there had been few like it on that part
of the coast for many years. Not even the barbecue,
last summer, when the humans roasted a whole sheep
over a log-fire down on the beach, and the little waves
came dancing rosily into the firelight, like elves on
tiptoe to smell the savory smoke of it; not even that
barbecue could compare with the banquet by the silver birch logs. Political life prevents the Skunk from
taking too much exercise. That is why his liver is so
attractive to Horned Owls.

In his excitement at the gleeful spectacle, Grandfather Grizzle leapt on to the roof of Blueberry Cottage, caught the dead Weasel by the tail, and flung
him down to Bubo, lest he should forget his dessert.

It was improbable that anyone would want dessert after a feast like that; but, if Bubo felt so disposed, the more of these titbits that he could demolish the better.

This thoughtful little act accomplished, Grizzle ran to the hole by the chimney, and entered, with amazing alacrity for one of his age, calling:

"Cosy! Curly! Rufus! Ruff! Where are you?"

Well he might ask. There was no sign of them anywhere. The room was not so devastated as he might have expected from the awful sounds he had heard. The floor near the chimney was littered with fragments of the big flower vases that used to stand so solidly on the stone mantelpiece. A chair was overturned. The feathers from the down cushions were scattered in all directions. There were some of the Butcher-bird's feathers among them, and a few red stains on the hearth. These made Grizzle very uneasy indeed. He wondered if the family had not been a preliminary course to the great feast outside.

"Curly! Cosy! Ruff! Rufus!" he called again. "Where *are* you?"

A thin ghostly little voice, curiously muffled, answered him from he could not tell where . . . "All right, Grandfather! Coming down!"

There was a scrattling sound, inside the chimney; a soft fall of soot on the hearth; and down, with three other separate falls of soot, Mr. and Mrs. Squirrel, followed by Curly, tumbled into the room. They had been halfway up the chimney. A pretty sight they were, too, as they stood before the astonished Grizzle, like three little chimneysweeps, black from head to foot—not to speak of their tails, which were exactly like the bushy brooms that twirl through the chimney-pots. They were about to embrace their grandfather when he hastily stepped aside.

"Stand back," he said, "you're making me sneeze."

"Wait a minute," said Mrs. Squirrel, who as we have often seen was extraordinarily practical. She ran upstairs on the silver birch balustrade, followed by Mr. Squirrel and Curly.

"Where are you going now?" called Grizzle, as though he supposed they would be looking for another and blacker chimney.

"Best bedroom," answered Mrs. Squirrel, "to rub the soot off, of course"; and they all three went into the room.

"How?" called Grandfather Grizzle.

"Lovely blankets up here," replied Mrs. Squirrel. "We're rolling in them!"

"Splendid," called Grandfather Grizzle. He was relieved to find the family more sensible for once than he had expected. He went over to the chimney-corner where he kept his acorns. They were all there. He popped one into his mouth and sat down to wait, quietly chewing. In a few minutes the Squirrels were down again, looking quite clean and well-groomed.

"I think I reckernize you now," said Grizzle. "You look almost like red squirrels to me."

"You should see the blankets," said Mrs. Squirrel. "Black isn't the word for them."

"Well. That's what they're for," said Grandfather Grizzle. "Might as well be used." Then, suddenly, he stopped chewing.

"Where's Ruff?" he said.

II

THE CROW'S NEST

SOLO WOKE EARLY the next morning in a fragrant world of dark-green pine and deep-blue sea; a world of washing waves and clamoring sea-gulls; where nothing, it seemed, could ever go wrong. He lit his fire in his usual cooking-place between two sheltering rocks where no sparks could catch the brushwood. Fir-cones and little boughs of silver birch were the kindling, with pine and driftwood on top. As soon as the fire was well alight he took a plunge into a deep rock-cove, where the water looked like liquid sapphire and was so deliciously cold that it made him burn from head to foot. Then he sat in the blazing sun to dry, and fished for his breakfast, while a song-sparrow piped good luck to him, and *very merry cheer.*

In five minutes he had a couple of flounders frying in his pan; and on such a morning if there is anything better for the nostrils than the blue smoke of crackling fir-cones and the smell of the breakfast frying, it must be far to seek. Solo, in any case, was not seeking it before he had finished his breakfast.

He began with a long drink of cold water from the spring. He followed it with a large bowl of oatmeal porridge, sweetened with a creamy layer of condensed milk from a tin. The milk was called Swiss on the tin; but, if you looked carefully, you saw in very small letters, at the bottom of the label, the truthful words —*Manufactured in Oklahoma*. He followed this luscious mixture with the two flounders, crisp and brown and spluttering from the pan; several equally crisp and brown corn muffins; about a pint of blueberries; and, also sweetened and made creamy by the truth from Oklahoma, two large cups of steaming hot coffee.

One of the things about Solo which the village boys didn't understand was his passion for colors. He would waste a whole hour poring over the pattern on a butterfly's wing. He would sit cross-legged in the grass outside his mother's cottage, crooning with delight over the way in which lozenges of color on the wings of the tortoiseshell blended and answered one another, like notes in music. At such times, if some of the supposedly sensible folk in the village saw him, they would shake their heads rather sorrowfully, or give his mother a sympathetic look, and go away without speaking; for they really thought that only a lad who was very queer indeed would behave like that.

As soon as he had finished his breakfast, therefore, though not a moment earlier, he remembered the exquisitely colored rosary of wampum which the Indian Sagamore had given him last night for Father Francis. He hardly expected to find it by day. It was too like the gifts that came through the Ivory Gate when he was asleep. He went to the bow of the canoe, where he *thought* he had carefully put it away; and—nothing was there; nothing but the scarf on which he thought he had laid it, and the coiled wet rope which he sometimes used for a mooring.

Curiously enough, now that it had gone, he felt almost certain that it had been there. The scarf was exactly where he thought he had placed it.

It was very odd, too, how the lovely forms of the shells, every tiniest whorl and curl, came back to him, with every gleam of the iridescent colors that had held him breathless in the moonlight. Dreams play odd tricks, of course. He remembered dreaming once of waves breaking against the rocks of Pooduck, and wondering, when he woke, how it was possible for him to see the irised colors in the spray; or to imagine those innumerable flying drops of water all at once, and make them into a picture for himself. So it *might* have been a dream; and yet he really felt he had lost something. He would have given everything he had to be able to take that Indian gift to Father Francis. It would be foolish, however, to grieve about something which perhaps never existed at all; and, though Solo might seem queer, he was far from foolish.

Perhaps it was because of the dream-colors that had been lost, that the sky and sea around Pooduck seemed so marvelous to him that October morning. He climbed on to a rock above the water, drawing a long breath, as if he could drink the colors in like some magical wine.

In this vivid air the white clouds looked almost crisp enough to carry a child—or a squirrel—through the sky. There was none of the mistiness of dreams; but he was haunted by a mystery behind this beautiful daylight world. He was teased by a curious tune that kept coming into his head and breaking off just where he wanted most to remember it. He wondered if he had really heard it last night; or whether it was only an echo of the song he had heard that other night with the Squirrels; and whether these were really the words:

Happy the child, when the chickadee sings to him!
Happy the hunter whose feet were as wings to him!
Up the wild glen, for a handful of blueberries!
Pick where you please, but beware of the dewberries!

Fill me a basket, and back to the tent with it
Light was their laugh on the wind, and they . . .

It had gone; like the footprints that Ruff and the rest had failed to trace. Perhaps, if he didn't try to remember, it would come back. The world around him was too beautiful and clear-cut this morning for mysteries. He saw the violet shadow of wings on the smooth stone at his feet, when the white gulls wheeled above him. He saw the green reflections of the pine trees in the limpid tide below; the peacock-blue of the deeper water, half a mile away; and, beyond that, the foam-fringed coast, with Blink Bonnie shining like a pearl among its darker pines; and the smouldering glory of the Maine woods on all the hills behind it.

Blueberry Cottage, being built of pine-logs, was not often seen so easily from Pooduck Island; but it was quite clear-cut this morning, and one of the glass panes in front, which had caught the sun, was blazing like a star.

Solo stood there for a long time. He wasn't thinking. He was only drinking it all in; but he was just as startled as if he had been absorbed in thought when he heard a quiet little cough behind him.

He turned quickly, but saw nothing to explain it at first.

"Ahem! Excuse me!" said the little voice. "I didn't want to interrupt; and, of course, I know you can swim; but have you noticed that the tide has now entirely surrounded your rock?"

Solo shaded his eyes under an arch of hand; and there he saw the owner of the voice. It was Ruff, perched on the bow of the canoe, like a mascot, carved in red cedar.

"How on earth?" cried Solo.

"It wasn't on earth," said Ruff. "It wasn't by sea, either. I came by air. The duck-hawk!"

"We'd better get back at once," said Solo. "They'll be worried about you at Blueberry Cottage."

"Not so worried as I am about *them*," said Ruff, breaking at once into a swift chirruping account of everything that had happened.

Solo quickly packed his camp-kit and the bucket of clams into the canoe, and while he was doing it he suddenly remembered something else. He was quite sure that last night he had left a small camp-knife in the bow, where he *thought* he had also left the wampum. The knife had a small steel chain, worn bright by its usual attachment to his hip-pocket, and it should have caught his eye at once. He searched everywhere for it; but it had vanished as completely as the dream-stuff.

"Lost something?" said Ruff.

"Knife," said Solo.

Ruff broke into a quiet chuckle that sounded like hickory nuts falling into the spring.

"*I* know who took it," he chirped. "Come, quick!"

Solo followed him up the white crumbly bank and across the little meadow to the clump of cedars.

"Look," said Ruff. He pointed to the fork of an

old tree, in which there was an accumulation of dead twigs which might once have been a nest.

Solo climbed up to the fork. As he reached it, a great crow rose from the cavity in the center, barking at him like an angry watch-dog.

"Old black thief," was all that Solo had time to reply; for the next moment he was staring at the loot in the old black thief's hiding place behind the barrier of dead twigs; and he rubbed his eyes as he looked at it, lest he should still be dreaming.

The treasure-trove included the following items:

1. Solo's knife with the steel chain.

2. Three brilliant feathers, which Jacopono himself might have worn in his tail.

3. A silver apostle spoon which the Reverend Ebenezer MacDoodle had tried to send his cook to jail for stealing.

4. A silver thimble, belonging to the cook, who firmly believed it had been appropriated by Mrs. MacDoodle.

5. A small pair of scissors, belonging to Mrs. Pringle at the Maple Inn, who was positive that Mrs. Willard Wall had slipped them into her reticule while admiring the dahlias in Mrs. Pringle's front parlor.

6. A shoe-buckle.

7. Various bits of colored glass beautifully rounded by the sea.

8. A small christening mug, believed to have been taken as a keepsake by a sorrowing relative, at the funeral of the oldest inhabitant, on finding that he had been forgotten in the will.

But, at the very center of this pirate hoard, there was something far more important to Solo—the rosary of wampum which the Indian Sagamore had given to him for Father Francis. Slowly, link by link, he drew it out of its dark ambush, with trembling fingers, as though he were drawing some wildly beautiful imagination out of the dusk of dreams into the sunlight of reality. He hung it round his neck, not because he thought that was the right place for so beautiful a thing, but to bring it down to the earth more safely.

All the other things which humans might value and could be restored to their owners he wrapped in a handkerchief, and fastened to his belt.

As he crossed the meadow, with Ruff running at his side, he touched the chain of wampum, shell by shell, thinking that the sunlight flowing through it was alive like the glow in the petals of a rose. It was their lucid colors and lovely forms that enchanted him. But there was more than that. There was one larger shell in the center, which he held up to his ear. He heard a soft whispering in it which, to the fanciful, might have been an echo of the sea or the sorrowful murmur of the Indian mother to whom it had once belonged. But it was really the whisper of his own heart.

He carried the birch-canoe down to the beach; set it afloat, and embarked in a kind of trance. At the first dip of the paddle, Ruff, who didn't like being too near the splashes, leapt on to Solo's bare shoulder and sat there, all the way across to the cove below Blink Bonnie, with his fur softly touching the cheek of his friend, or a quiet little whisk of his bushy tail when Solo was engaged too deeply with his thoughts to steer straight.

12

POODUCK ISLAND HAS AN EYE

I T WAS NOW that the real trouble for Solo began.
On the evening of his return from Pooduck
Island, he restored to their owners the various glittering articles which he had found in the crow's nest.
He noticed, at the time, that Mrs. Wall looked at him
oddly. Instead of thanking him, she called her husband to come and see what Solo had brought them.
"*Quite* a surprise, isn't it," she said. Then they both
looked at him oddly, and Willard Wall said, "Seems
to me I've heard that yarn about a crow *afore*. You
didn't find, or leave, anything else in that crow's nest,
I 'spose?"

Solo didn't in the least realize what was brewing for
him; but it was obvious enough that they were think-

ing something very unpleasant indeed, so he replied, "I left a few colored pebbles and an old shoe-buckle in the nest. The crow told me he'd be very much obliged if he might keep those, and he begged to apologize to Mrs. Wall and yourself for having given you so much trouble."

It was an unfortunate reply, perhaps, for it lent color to Willard Wall's remarks, later, when he quoted it to his cronies round the stove at the village store, and added, "if that ain't *queer*, I'd like to know what *is*."

If he had heard the yarn that Solo spun to Father Francis the same evening perhaps his wish would have been gratified; for the old padre had an extraordinary way of attracting Solo's confidence, and Solo told him the whole story of his adventure on Pooduck Island. He was very enthusiastic about the beautiful glimpse he had caught through that Eye in the wood. Father Francis watched him closely as he was talking. Solo went into a kind of rhapsody about it; and, to illustrate what he was saying, he made a little sketch of what he called the Eye of Pooduck. Father Francis looked at this closely, too; and then looked up at Solo again.

"You've done a good deal of work at Mr. Jacks' studio, haven't you?" he said.

"Odd jobs," said Solo.

"Does Mr. Jacks know that you can draw like this?" said Father Francis.

"I used to watch him at work. He taught me a lot

at the beginning; but he's gone now," said Solo. "I've been painting a little, too."

Mr. Jacks, in fact, had given Solo a lot of junk to burn one day—a broken palette, old canvases, brushes, twisted tubes, out of which, if you took a little trouble, colors could still be squeezed. "Get rid of 'em anyhow," Mr. Jacks had said. "Make a bonfire of 'em, down on the beach; or keep 'em and set up as an artist for yourself, if you like."

That, of course, was only Mr. Jacks' little joke. But Solo had taken him literally, and had kept the junk in his own bedroom, thereby distressing his mother, and, as she said, making the whole house smell of paint. Solo had made many experiments, in private, with his brushes and tubes of color. The results had only deepened his mother's own secret alarm over Solo's supposed queerness, and she was thankful that he had shown them to nobody—yet.

In the bare, very plainly furnished sitting-room at the padre's house, Solo always felt curiously at home. On one of the walls there was a steel engraving of St. Mark's and the Doge's Palace, at Venice. On another, an Arundel Society reproduction of the Sistine Madonna and Child. On another there was a *Flight into Egypt.* On the fourth wall there were shelves of books, among which Solo's eyes always wandered to the *Lives of the Painters,* translated from the Italian.

In fact, before the padre had entered the room, Solo had been examining one of these volumes, and had been reading about a shepherd boy named Giotto, who became a painter, and worked at Assisi, the home of another Francis. There was a curious story about some great personage wanting to see proof of Giotto's skill, whereupon Giotto drew a perfect circle with one sweep of his hand and said "show him *that*." Solo tried it himself on a piece of paper, which he had hurriedly shut up in the volume when Father Francis entered, but he had not had time to put the book back on the shelf.

"Would you like to take that book home with you, Solo?" said Father Francis.

Solo's face shone. "I would indeed," he said. "I'll take great care of it."

"I know you will," said the padre. "But there's something else I want you to do for *me*. I didn't quite understand what you were telling me about that window in the wood. It sounded very beautiful; but I wish you'd paint it for me, so that I could—look through it myself, and see exactly what you saw."

"I'll try," said Solo.

Father Francis picked up the book and before handing it over, took out the paper on which Solo had drawn his circle.

"What's this?" said Father Francis.

"It's what Grandfather Grizzle calls the Circum Ferrence," said Solo.

"Grandfather Grizzle! Circum Ferrence!" chuckled the padre. "Talk sense!"

"It's the O of Giotto," said Solo, gravely.

"O," said Father Francis, even more gravely. "I see."

But he didn't—*quite*—yet.

Solo went back, with the book under his arm, and set to work on his picture at once. He used the best of the canvases that had been given to him at the studio. He worked many hours a day on it, and it grew under his hand as though it were alive. His mother caught sight of it one morning and said, "What do you call *that?*"

Her mind was not eased when Solo replied,

"Pooduck Island has an Eye."

In the meantime, as a result of Willard Wall's hints, everything that had been lost or stolen in the village for months past was suddenly remembered, with kindly suggestions that it was probably hidden in the crow's nest, and that Solo himself was, of course, the real crow.

When the picture was ready, Solo wrapped a piece of old sailcloth around it, and carried it down the village street, on his way to Father Francis. He was accosted by Willard Wall, not far from the padre's door.

" 'Spose you couldn't show us where that crow's nest is," said Willard, while a gaping group of lads drew round to enjoy the baiting of one they called queer because he was so different from themselves. Solo was too proud to argue the matter, or to offer them evidence in proof of his tale. Perhaps he knew that, if he took them over to the island and let them poke their noses into the nest, it would only strengthen their conviction that he had put the things there himself. So again he answered, perhaps a little unfortunately:

"I *could* show you where it is; but it happens to be a strict secret between the crow and me."

"Between the crow and *me*," exclaimed Willard Wall, who was almost as good at pronouns as he was at detective work; and, like many of his kind, took a great delight in airing his imaginary ability to correct his betters. "Between you and *I*, my lad," he said loftily. "Between you and *I*, there's only one crow in Old Harbour, and that's a crazy crow that don't know how to place his words right, an' ought to be put where crazy crows belong."

"Ah, that's right! That's true enough!" said the on-lookers. "Look what he's carryin' now, under his arm. Let's have a look at it!"

They made a move towards him, as though to lay hands on his precious picture—precious because Father Francis wanted it—but he turned and faced them so fiercely that they fell back.

" 'Tain't safe to have a cuss like that goin' about," muttered Willard Wall. "There'll be murder done in this village, one of these dark nights."

"This parcel belongs to Father Francis," said Solo. "If anyone touches it, I'll—"

"Ah! Looks mighty like sumpin' belongin' to

Father Francis. Guess we'll see that parcel delivered," said Willard Wall.

Solo walked past him as though he were non-existent, and knocked at the door of the little house, next to the church. Father Francis himself opened the door.

"Good! You've brought it," he said, with obvious pleasure. Then, with a swift and curious glance at the gaping group on the sidewalk, he made way for Solo to pass into the house and closed the door in their faces.

"Guess he's been pinchin' sumpin' from Father Francis," was the general verdict outside.

Inside the house, a strangely different scene was taking place. Removing the wrapper of sailcloth, Solo disclosed an unframed canvas which he propped on a chair for Father Francis to examine. *"Pooduck Island has an Eye,"* he said.

At the first sight of it, Father Francis gave an excited exclamation. But he made no comment. No picture like that had ever been seen in Old Harbour before. It was itself like a window through which the light of another and more beautiful world streamed into the small bare room.

"How did you do it?" the old padre said at last.

"I did it for you," said Solo.

"Will you give me permission to do what I like with it?" said Father Francis.

"It's not mine. It's yours," said Solo.

"Very well," said Father Francis. "For the present,

we'll leave it at that. By-the-bye, after you'd gone last week, I measured that 'Circum Ferrence,' as you called it, and found it was a perfect circle. I suppose you used compasses, or something, didn't you?"

"Of course not," said Solo, rather indignantly.

"You mean—"

"It was the O of that artist I was reading about— Giotto," said Solo, as though he were giving a pass-word.

"O," said Father Francis again. "I *see.*"

And this time he really did see.

13

THE IMPORTANCE OF SQUIRRELS

THE DAYS WERE GROWING shorter now. Winds went howling through the forest, and sent the autumn leaves flying like flocks of gorgeous birds. The pines looked darker and richer by the side of their stripped companions, the lean poplar, and the leafless maple; while the silver birch, against the darkness of the pines, was more than ever the shining Spirit of the Woods. The nights were growing longer. The first snow had already fallen. Solo had seemed less happy of late. He came more often to Blueberry Cottage in these long winter evenings, as though it were a kind of escape. He liked the company of the Squirrels more and more, though the only conversation might be the crackling of the pine-cones in the fire, or the rattling of a shutter in the wind. He was more and more wrapped up in his drawing; and sometimes he would bring his paint-brushes and tubes of color. Ruff and Curly were greatly interested in these tubes, and though they were none the wiser for it, Solo would tell them the names of the colors as he squeezed them out or made little flowery patches with them on his palette. They made a game of it.

"That's *Ash-of-Roses*," he would say.

"Like the sky at evening," Ruff would chirrup.

"*Crimson—*"

"Like clover in midsummer," Curly would murmur.

"*Cobalt blue—*"

"Like the sky at night, when there are no clouds," Ruff would answer.

"*Dark purple—*"

"Heartsease by Blink Bonnie, of course," Curly would say.

"*Orange—*"

"Marygolds . . . dandelions . . . devil's paint-brushes . . . angry sunsets," they would both chirp alternately.

"*Pale green—*"

"Young beech-leaves . . . fern crumples . . . grass in April." That would be one to Ruff and two to Curly.

"*Chinese white—*"

"Foam under the pines . . . a sea-gull's wing . . . crest of a wave . . . cherry blossom . . . sails at sea." That was five, to Curly.

"*Ultramarine—*"

"The sea round Pooduck Island, on August after-noons," said Ruff, who went by the color, of course, not by the word.

"Pale blue—"

"Shadow of wings on snow in sunlight . . . shadow of naked trees on snow . . ." said Curly, almost as though it were a song.

"Yellow—"

"Patch of mustard-blossom in spring," said Ruff, very quickly; and, as he said it, Solo's eyes darkened, for—very far away—he seemed to hear that mysterious voice again, going through the woods and saying in tones that none of the others would hear or under-stand:

"It is like a grain of mustard-seed, which a man took, and cast into his garden; and it grew, and waxed a great tree; and the fowls of the air lodged in the branches of it."

But it was the tubes and the palette and the brushes —especially the brushes—that interested Ruff and Curly. What Solo drew and painted he usually kept to himself. He didn't invite them to look at it as a rule; and as the Squirrels had a great respect for his feelings, they usually pretended not to notice what he was doing on his drawing-board or canvas.

Grandfather Grizzle, in fact, used to take the oppor-tunity of drawing Solo out on all sorts of questions that interested or puzzled him about the world in general.

One evening, when they were expecting their relations, the Chipmunks, to supper, the questions were very puzzling indeed. The discussion began with a very sage remark by Grandfather Grizzle.

" 's a big world, Solo!"

" 'Tis indeed, Grizzle," replied Solo, without looking up from his drawing.

"Almos' too big to handle, I reckon," the old fellow went on, chewing reflectively.

"Seems like it, Grizzle. But p'raps it looks bigger to humans and squirrels than really 'tis."

"Mebbe. 'Pears too big for most anything. Seems as if folks don't count in it at all. 'Spose they do, Solo?"

Solo looked at Grizzle with his eyes growing deep in that curious way they had.

"I guess we all count, Grizzle."

"Don't s'pose we Squirrels amount to much. Do you, Solo?"

"Why, yes! I reckon Squirrels are mighty important. There's a whole oak forest over by Blue Hill that wouldn't be there at all, if it hadn't been for the Squirrels, a couple of hundred years ago."

"How come, Solo?"

"Well, you see, they buried their acorns, and forgot all about 'em."

"Kind of careless, I call that, Solo."

"All the same," replied Solo, "they planted an oak forest; and ships have been built with the timber from it. It's like a very long chain of things one leading to another. But those ships, in a way, were made by the Squirrels, too."

"S'pose they were. But, after that, where did the ships go?"

"Mostly to Europe, I guess."

"Ah—place where the humans kill one another as if humans didn't count neither. Millions of 'em, ain't it, Solo?"

"Millions upon millions, Grizzle."

"Kind of wasteful seems to me. 'Pears like we Squirrels are jus' tools. Don't know what we're doin', none of us!"

"Maybe somebody else knows. Maybe your oaks, and your ships, may be saving more'n you guess. As for bein' tools—it takes a lot of time and trouble to make good tools, 'specially tools that can work of 'emselves, with eyes and ears like yours, Grizzle. And, mind you, can begin the work two hundred years beforehand. But I s'pose we shan't understand everything till we come to the end of the world."

"I agree with Solo," said Mr. Squirrel, rather primly. "We must take the long view, you know."

"Hope the view ain't goin' to be too lawng," said Grizzle. "End of the world's a mighty way off."

"And that Mrs. MacDoodle's been promised her fur coat for *this* winter," said Mrs. Squirrel, biting off a thread in the work upon which she was engaged.

"True," said Mr. Squirrel, more primly than ever, "But that, in a sense, *actually* confirms what Solo says about the value and importance of Squirrels." Rufus had rather a habit of "agreeing" with Solo, even when he didn't understand him; for he liked to be on the winning side in an argument. "After all," he continued, "it is not the *individual* Squirrel that matters. We may lose our skins, but we *do* make our little contribution to the Whole. It would be a poor spirit indeed, if we looked for personal advantages in a world as big as this."

"That's exactly why I married you," said Cosy, snapping her scissors within an inch of his nose, and seriously endangering his precious little whiskers. "And I only hope that somebody is on the watch for Mrs. MacDoodle's skin, though all you could make of it would be kettle-drums. And wouldn't I whack 'em if I had the chance!"

"I quite agree that squirrel skins are more valuable, my dear," returned her spouse. "Willard Wall, as we know, has been promised a nickel and a half for any of our skins that he can get. But that again confirms what Solo and I have been saying."

"A nickel and a half's big money, I know," said Grandfather Grizzle. "Leastways, it would be for *your* skin, Rufus. But I'd give a lot more'n that, if I had it, to keep Ruff and Curly the way they are now. Shouldn't feel 'tall the same way about 'em if Mrs. MacDoodle was takin' 'em to meeting every Sunday in her fur coat. Mebbe that's some folks idee of *heaven*. 'Tain't mine. Sooner have the chimney-corner in

Blueberry Cottage and my own li'l pile of hickory nuts, an' Ruff and Curly talkin' nonsense, an' Rufus takin' lawng views by a pine-log fire. Guess Rufus can take his lawng views here better'n he could in Mrs. MacDoodle's fur coat, even if it do take him to meetin' Sundays."

"Don't worry about Rufus, Grandfather," said Mrs. Squirrel. "He's been talking to those owls in the barn. They've been trying to give him an outline of every-thing. Long views indeed. I know what *that* ends in."

Solo just caught the word 'chipmunks,' and thought that Rufus was expressing a quiet doubt about *their* value in the world. So he broke into the conversation, and gave his own opinion:

"*I* think the Chipmunks are mighty important, too," he said.

"So do *we*," piped two lively little voices near the roof. Two bright-eyed Chipmunks had just entered by the private door, the secret of which had been en-trusted to them, as cousins.

"Hello, Mr. Chippy! Hello, Mrs. Chippy," cried Ruff and Curley. "Come down and join us!" And, quicker than winking, the two little cousins, in their beautiful fur coats of golden brown, with the five black stripes down their backs, were seated in the chimney-corner, one on each side of Grandfather Grizzle.

"Waal, Chippy, glad to see you," said the old fellow. "Glad to see you, too, Mrs. Chippy. You're lookin' fine. How's things over at Blue Hill?"

"Couldn't be better," said Mrs. Chippy. "Of course, it's almost time for us to begin our winter sleep; but we thought we must come over and see you before the big snow falls."

"Came just at the right moment, too, Mrs. Chippy. Glad you heard that li'l compliment from Solo 'bout your fam'ly. Goes a lawng way back, your fam'ly, I guess."

"There's an old family tradition," said Mr. Chippy, in a very pleasant and musical little voice, "that we Chipmunks once lived in a gigantic and very beautiful valley, so far to the West that it was entirely surrounded by sunset clouds."

"Polar myth," said Mr. Squirrel, in a peculiarly superior tone.

"Now, what do you mean by *that,* pray?" said Mr. Chippy, rather indignantly.

"The legend of your beautiful valley, so conveniently far away that nobody can go and see it, is a very old one," replied Mr. Squirrel. "The best opinion among the Eastern Squirrels is that it belongs to the realms of *polar myth.* That, I believe, is the proper phrase—*polar myth.*"

"Hope you're right this time, my dear," said Mrs. Squirrel. "The last time you said it you called it *molar pith.*"

Mr. Squirrel winced.

Solo was trying to look serious, but found it difficult, because somebody or something seemed to be whistling an absurd rhyme through the key-hole of the front door. To the others, on this occasion, it was only the night wind, explaining how lonely it was; but to Solo it sounded very like that mysterious stranger who had gone through the wood singing the song of Silly James. Solo often heard him when others couldn't. Sometimes he was sad, and sometimes he made Solo laugh; and this, perhaps, was what made some of the humans think him queer. It came in a fantastic whistle tonight:

The Man who left Athens and went to the Birds,
Had a very fine sense of the meaning of words.
He said that the place of the Birds was a Pole
Which stuck through the center of things and could
*   roll.*
But I think that the world would be more like a hole
Or a tunnel, perhaps, to the underground mole;
While, as for the bat, in the ellum-tree bole,
Since he hangs upside down, it would look very droll;
And exceedingly flat to the flounder and sole;
Very flat, I should say, to the sole.

"*Molar pith* was what Rufus said before," said Grizzle, offering his bag of acorns to the Chipmunks. "I prefer *molar pith*. Have some?"

"The fact remains," Mr. Squirrel said desperately, "the best opinion in the East now regards the giant valley in the sunset-clouds as a fable. It's one of those beautiful legends belonging to the childhood of the world."

"O, but *do* let's hear it then," exclaimed Ruff and Curly together.

"By all means," said Mr. Squirrel, with the most exasperating politeness, "we should all allow our minds to relax, at times."

"Relax on *that*, then," said Mrs. Squirrel, sticking the point of her needle into his tail. Mr. Squirrel gave one sharp little cry and decided that he had better be a good listener.

14

THE LEGEND OF THE CHIPMUNK

"WELL," SAID MR. CHIPPY, "it will be best to begin again from the beginning. It is *said* that, in the old days, the Chipmunks inhabited a gigantic and very beautiful valley in the West, where the sun goes down. It had tremendous walls of naked rock on either side, and a river as green as the young leaves of a poplar flowing through it. The floor of the valley was of young green grass as fine and soft as mole skin. Mushrooms and currants and raspberries grew in the meadowy spaces between the woods; and there were dogwoods with fruit like the strawberry; and acorns of five different kinds; and cones of spruce and fir such as the East has never known for the fine flavor of their seeds. There were the soft blue leaves of ju-

135

niper and wild red plum trees; and indeed whole forests in which all the fruits and nuts that the Chipmunks like best grew in the most profuse—er—"

"Profusion," suggested Mr. Squirrel, looking as if he were repentant, but really trying to lead Mr. Chippy down that valley, so to speak.

"Thank you, Rufus," said Mr. Chippy. "Exactly what I was trying to say. *In the most profuse profusion.*" This was really polite of Mr. Chippy, for he knew that 'profusion' was not the best word when he had already said "profuse."

"There were beautiful waterfalls," he continued, "which seemed, from a distance, to come slowly flowing down the great cliffs from the sunset-sky, bringing all its colors with them. One of these was called the Bridal Veil. They made a sound like drowsy bees and kept the valley cool and green in the hottest of summers, but if you stood near them, some of them were rushing cataracts, as tremendous as they were beautiful. Their spray went up like a mist over the tallest tree-tops, and watered a hundred open glades of all kinds of flowers. It was a canyon of Paradise; and it all belonged to the Chipmunks, the Golden Hopis, who were known afterwards among the humans as the good stewards of the Happy Valley."

"Weren't there any other creatures in it?" said Curly.

"Indeed, there were," said Mr. Chippy. "There were birds with dark crests and bright blue wings that fluttered through the branches like bits of the sky.

They were called blue jays. There were plump black bears that lived on honeycomb and climbed the trees with their cubs; and sometimes an Indian tribe would encamp by the river. But they did not kill in that valley; and the deer, with their kind dark eyes, would come up to the tents and eat the maize out of the hands of the Indian children. For they all knew it was the kingdom of the Chipmunks, the good stewards. It was theirs because of the heroic deed that one of them had done there."

He paused a moment, looked at Mr. Squirrel very firmly, and then continued:

"You must know there was a great mystery about the walls of that valley, and how they came to be so high; or, if you prefer it, how the valley came to be so deep. The owls said that the river had been made by the valley. The moles declared that the valley had been made by the river, which had slowly gnawed its way down through the rocks, like the saws with which the foresters cut through a fallen tree."

"I've seen them," nodded Ruff. "But somebody had to hold the saw."

Mr. Chippy gave Ruff a courteous little bow, and continued.

"Others said that if a river could cut so great a gash in the earth, it would one day cut the whole way through, and the earth would fall apart, like an apple divided by a knife. But the wiser ones declared that none of these things was the real cause. They said

that the walls grew and the river flowed to a musical in-
cantation; and that if you sat very still on the tree-tops
and half-closed your eyes, the sunset clouds would
cease to move. Then you would see the cliffs quietly
growing up against them, very slowly, as the leaves
change their colors in the fall. Sometimes, if you
were not watching them, the growth might be quicker;
and, in the changes of the year, the Chipmunks often
came upon a great rock that they had not noticed before, though their eyes were the keenest in the valley.

"One evening, an Indian woman, encamping with
her tribe, near the river, wrapped her baby in a shawl
and laid it in the smooth hollow of a low rock, where
she thought it would be raised above the damp ground,
and sleep soundly at her side all night. But, while she
slept, the rock began to grow quietly upward. All
through the hours of darkness it grew upward and upward, till it was higher than the cliffs on either side,
and had veiled its head in the clouds. And when she
awoke in the morning it was a monstrous column of
sheer rock, towering above her into the sky; and, when
it stood clear of the clouds, she could see the dark red
fringe of the Indian shawl, in which she had wrapped
her child, fluttering against the blue.

"She called to her tribe, wildly, and they gathered
round her in amazement; but the scarp was so sheer
and the height so vast that none could climb it or find
a foothold. She would have called on the eagle to help
her in her desperation, but the eagle might have car-

ried the child to his own eyrie. It was then that the
Chipmunk, of whom she had never thought, came into
his kingdom.

"He came out of the woods, our little father, the
Chipmunk, and looked up at the rock and the weeping
mother; and he crept up to her and whispered, between the plaits of her long hair, while she bowed her
head upon her knees and wept. In a very small voice
he whispered: *Do not weep. I will help you.*

"And she looked up and saw him, and clasped him
with her hands, and looked again at him, and held him
to her heart, sobbing and laughing. Then he whispered to her again; and running from tent to tent, like
one distraught, she gathered all the thinnest thread she
could find and knotted it together. One end of it she
looped around the neck of the Chipmunk and across
his breast; for this was what he had told her to do when
he whispered between the long plaits of her hair—*'I
will help you.'*

"Then the Chipmunk, our little father, looked up at
the great rock, and saw how tremendous it was, and
himself so small beside it, and he looked at the mother
again, and the wild hope in her face; and he knew that
though the rock was great his own heart was greater.
So he went up to the base of the rock and laid his heart
against its hardness, and stretched up his hands, our
little father; and with that loop of thin thread over one
shoulder and around his heart, he began the upward
way.

"And in the first hour of his going up, there was hardly a crack or a splinter on which even those small hands and feet could lay hold or rest. At one time he would gain an inch and slip back three. At another, he would slip back half an inch and gain four; so that, in all, he would be only an inch and a half nearer to the sky. Yet, in that hour, when it was all added together, he climbed a tenth of the terrible upward way.

"But at the end of that hour, his heart failed him; for suddenly the rock overhung his head; and unless he had been a fly, it was impossible for him to climb outwards and over it. Every sinew in his body was aching. There was blood on his hands and feet. His nerves quivered, and his fingers lost their strength and shook. He clung to the sheer face of the rock, and saw the ground far below him where he must fall in a little while. And slowly, slowly, his fingers lost their grip; and, at last, he loosened them, thinking it was the end.

"But he did not fall. For the thin thread that was looped around his heart by the Indian mother had caught on a tiny thorn-shoot and—so strangely do all things work together—it held him till his strength began to return.

"And when it came back, he looked up again at the rock which overhung his head. He knew that he could not pass that way. But he did not think of returning to the ground. He said to himself, *I will try the other side;* and he lifted the loop of thread from the thorn, and worked his way round to the other side of the monstrous column. And all the Indian tribe on the ground below went round to the other side to watch; the tribe to see how soon he would fall, but the mother to watch him, inch by inch, go higher. And suddenly to the amazement of the tribe, they saw him running up the face of the rock as though it had been no more than a giant redwood; for the Chipmunk our little father, had found a crevice so small that it could not be seen from below. It went almost all the way to the crest, among the clouds; and he went up with it, all the way, till again, at the very last foot of the ascent, the rock grew out over his head, so that only a fly could have overcome it; and this time, it was the same on all sides of the column. It thrust out over his head everywhere, for nearly a yard.

"Then, at the moment when all hope died, he saw fluttering above and beyond him, against the blue sky, the dark red fringe of the Indian shawl in which the child was wrapped. It was a yard away from his head outwards over the abyss, and he had no foot-hold from which to leap, but he thought, *I will make the best foot-hold I can.* So he worked with his feet till he had loosened a few grains of the rock, and got a little better foot-hold. It was not much; but it was a little better; and then he looked up at the sky above him and the green valley below him, and said 'good-bye' to them, and leapt up and outwards . . . *and missed.*

"It was only by a hair's breadth that his hands failed to reach the dark-red fringe, for the tips of his fingers touched it; but he missed. He was in the air, up and out over the abyss . . . yet, he did not fall.

"He never knew what happened; but he *thought* that the hand of the Great Spirit caught him as he began to fall. It was unseen—that hand of light; but it caught him and held him and drew him gently on to the crest of the rock, and laid him there by the sleeping Indian child. It was then, only then, that our little father, looking on the face of the child, asleep in the sunlight, felt the movement of tears, aching up from his heart to his little dry throat, and coming at last to his eyes.

"The tribe below him could see nothing of this; and even when he had reached the crest, they still told the mother that her hope was hopeless. For how could a Chipmunk carry a child down that precipice to the earth, or how could a thin thread bear the weight of a child? But the mother paid no heed to them; for our little father, the Chipmunk, had whispered into her ear, and told her what to do.

"She gathered together all the bow-strings of the tribe and, knotting them together into a single cord, she tied one end of it to the thin thread. She gave a little tug to the thread, as a fish in the depths of the sea might tug at a line; but the Chipmunk, our little father, among the clouds, felt it as a little tug at his own heart, and—inch by inch, foot by foot, slowly and carefully, he pulled the thread up until he laid hold upon the stronger cord. While he was doing this the

The tribe refused to believe the child could be saved.

mother gathered together all the ropes of the tents, and knotting them together into a single rope, she tied one end of this to the cord of the bow-strings. And the Chipmunk slowly drew this also up, with the mother helping him from below, until he held the rope of ropes. And still the tribe, so far below in the valley, refused to believe that the child could be saved; for how—though the rope be ever so strong—how could a Chipmunk let down a human child to safety. The wisest man in the tribe proved this, to the comfort of his own heart; for without knowing it, he wished it to be over. He proved it, point by point, to the mother, touching the tops of his fingers before her and watching curiously—as only the wise ones can watch—for the hope in her face to die. But the mother said nothing; for the wise man did not know what our little father, the Chipmunk, had whispered to her. She said nothing; but she went on knotting more tent-ropes together and tying them to the end of the strong rope till it was long enough to reach the earth on both sides of the rock.

"Then, while the mother held one end of the rope below, on the north side of the rock, the Chipmunk fastened the other end around the child, and took it across the smooth top of the rock, and lowered the child down very gently, on the south side. But it was the mother, on the earth below, who held the weight, and kept the rope sliding slowly and very carefully through her hands.

"And to prevent the child being frightened, our little father, the Chipmunk, came down with it, holding on to the rope above its head and chirruping little songs to it as they swung over the abyss. And the little one crowed and smiled at him all the way back to the earth.

"Then the Indian mother caught the child in her arms and wept and laughed over it; and the tribe gathered round her, and told her that the little one must be set apart for some great purpose; and when all the weeping and laughter and talk was finished, she looked round for the Chipmunk to thank him. But our little father had gone quietly away, taking with him in remembrance only one of the dark-red strands from the Indian shawl."

Mr. Chippy paused here and looked once more at Rufus, for a full half-minute. Then, in a very quiet voice, he continued:

"There are some who would say that the hand which caught our little father in mid-air and drew him on to the rock belongs to the realm of fable or, as Rufus would say, '*myth*.' But—from that day onwards, our little father, and all the Chipmunks, have carried on their golden-brown coats the five beautiful stripes where the outstretched fingers of light had so beautifully imprinted their own dark shadow."

There was a long silence. Then Mr. Squirrel nervously moistened his lips and prepared to say something; but he put it in the form of a question this time.

"Do you think there can be any truth in such a story, Solo?" he asked.

"Fables, and parables, have been used to tell the truth for hundreds of years," said Solo.

"Then you admit it *is* a fable?" said Mr. Squirrel.

"Yes"; said Solo, "if *you'll* admit that fables often tell the truth."

Mr. Squirrel clasped his head with both hands. He was an honest little creature, and he really couldn't see what Solo meant; but he did see, out of the corner of his eye, that Mrs. Squirrel had another needle ready.

"I wish I could see it," he said. "I suppose you couldn't explain it a little?"

Solo thought for a moment. "Ever looked through a telescope, Rufus?"

"No."

"If you look through the little eye of a telescope, you can see ships on the horizon that no human eye, or Squirrel's eye, could see. It's a kind of concentrated picture; but you must focus it just right or you'll see nothing but a blur. Maybe fables, and parables, and pictures, and poems, are like the pictures of the telescope, which you can't see any other way because the distances are too big. Nobody can see all the way from Squirrels dropping acorns to those ships' timbers we were talking about. But you can see it in a poem about Squirrels building ships."

Solo might just as well have been talking to himself,

of course; but he held up the picture on which he had been working. Mr. Squirrel blinked at it.

"D'you see anything there, Rufus?" said Solo.

"It's just wet paint to me," he said, "a nice little mess of wet paint."

"Do *you* see anything?" Solo said, holding the picture up to Curly.

"It's Pooduck Island, from the shore by Blink Bonnie," she said, at once. "It's beautiful, Solo."

"*And* absolutely true," said Mr. Chippy, looking over her shoulder.

"Could you tell the time of day by it?" said Solo.

"One hour before sunset," said Mr. Chippy.

"When the wind goes down, and the water looks all sleeky and smooth," said Curly.

"Right," said Solo. "That's exactly when I saw it. Curious, isn't it, Rufus?"

Mr. Squirrel was honestly astonished; though, once or twice before, he had been puzzled to find that Curly could see her own face quite clearly in a forest pool, and indeed would spend a quarter of an hour studying it, while he could see nothing of his own but bits of broken color.

"And now, Rufus," said Solo, "do you mind if *I* ask a question? Is it really the opinion of the Barn Owls that the gigantic and beautiful valley in the West never existed?"

"I'm afraid so," said Mr. Squirrel. "I hate destroying cherished beliefs. But I'm afraid so."

"Sorry," said Solo. "I know it's too far for you to go and see it; but my mother was born there. It's called the Yosemite. Her father was one of the rangers. P'raps that's why I've always hoped to visit it one day. There's a mountain that looks like a great Stone Face asleep, which I should like to paint."

"Anything more to say, Rufus," said Mrs. Squirrel, putting her needle away. "If so, I should keep it till after supper. *I* agree with Solo."

15

SOLO'S TROUBLE

ON A FINE FROSTY EVENING, some weeks later, Solo and the whole Squirrel family were gathered around the log-fire which he had lighted for them. Nobody ever passed Blueberry Cottage after nightfall in the winter, so there was no danger, they thought, of the sharpest human nose detecting the smell of wood-smoke; and all the Squirrels were feeling very happy. Lately, they had not been sure that all was going well with Solo, among the humans. He seemed to have something on his mind; and, this evening, although nobody could have been a more welcome guest, he had certainly surprised them by saying that he wanted to stay the night, and sleep on the floor near the hearth. This was one reason why they were all sitting up later than usual; and they were glad to notice that the friendly chatter of their fireside made Solo look more cheerful. But they couldn't help wondering what the trouble could be.

There had been many improvements since we last saw the family together, and they were now most comfortably settled for the winter. The small door through the partition into the verandah had been successfully nibbled out. It looked quite as artistic as the holes that humans cut in houses for the use of hens; and Solo had swept up the bits, chuckling over the surprise the humans would feel at this neatness when they returned. Quite deliberately, he had taken a tiny brush and tray from an old doll's house in a cupboard and laid them by the hole, with a few crumbs of the nibbled wood in the tray, so that Mrs. Squirrel might at least obtain credit for tidiness on this occasion. He had fixed the entrance in the roof, so that nothing larger than a squirrel could now get through it; and he had also made a new and cunning little door which slid in a groove and would baffle anyone who didn't know the trick.

Grandfather Grizzle sat chewing in his usual chimney-corner, facing the picture of the squirrel, which the family—to his annoyance—now accepted as his portrait. He shifted his plug of acorn.

"That picture's been there too long," he said. "I don't like it. Humans don't understand squirrels."

"Solo does," said Curly.

"Solo ain't a human," said Grizzle.

Solo was sitting a little way back from the group, silently watching them, and doing something with colored chalks on a white board. From time to time he would look up at Grandfather Grizzle and then look back at what he was doing with his chalks; so he wasn't paying much attention to the conversation. But he chuckled at this last remark, and said, "I can tell you what I read in a big human book about Squirrels, if you like. Can't say it was flattering."

At this, of course, the whole Squirrel family was agog to know exactly what had been said about them.

"Well," said Solo, "the Author—mind you, he was only a human—said you were, all of you, terrible chatterers."

There was silence, for a moment.

"I like that," said Mrs. Squirrel. "I remember sitting in a chestnut tree, outside the schoolhouse, last Spring, and listening to the female humans at a jumble-sale. Starlings were nothing to it."

"Gosh," said old Grizzle, "when I lived in the—er—"

"Circles," said Mrs. Squirrel, determined to be right this time.

"Chimney," the old fellow replied, perversely. "You should have heard the chatter in that studio. Couldn't hear yourself cracking a hickory nut!"

"The cheek of calling *us* chatterers!" Curly broke in. "You mean a *human* actually said that, in *print?*"

"In *print*," said Solo, "and in a book weighing about four times as heavy as you and Ruff together."

"That's very interesting," said Mr. Squirrel loftily, "in view of the fact that—when it suits them—they call all of us who are not human 'dumb animals.' They pride themselves on that distinction. As for their print, why, it's nothing but a way of listening to silent chatter when nobody is there. Indeed, they've invented a machine now which will actually chatter in an empty room. They turn knobs and listen to what they call 'important announcements.' I've heard several. One of them was about razor-blades. They sang that—to something they call music. It sounded like Willard Wall's cow looking for her calf."

"I looked through a window at Blink Bonnie, once," said Curly, "when Mrs. MacDoodle was giving a tea-party. Everybody was talking at once, and what d'you think *they* were talking about? They were actually talking about something called 'the talkies.' "

"Ay, I know," said Grandfather Grizzle. "When they've exhausted theirselves by talkin' with their own mouths, they go and sit in a big dark cellar—hundreds of 'em—and listen to pictures of other humans talkin' and havin' conniption fits. Talkin'. I've heard 'em yellin' and screamin' blue murder, and enjoying it, mind you. Queer critters!"

"Nobody objects to their enjoying themselves in their own odd way," said Mr. Squirrel. "But it really *is* going a *little* far to call *us* 'chatterers,' on top of it."

"I was afraid you wouldn't like it," said Solo. "There was a lot more. But I'd better not repeat it."

"O, yes, *do* tell us," said Mrs. Squirrel. "Please don't think we really mind. *I* think it's frightfully *amusing,* don't you, Rufus?"

"I think it is *rah-thah* interesting," drawled Mr. Squirrel. "It may lead to a better understanding between our respective peoples if we know exactly how we appear to one another."

"Well," said Solo, "this human writer says that the Squirrels are inveterate scolds, and will often follow another creature for miles into the woods for the mere satisfaction of abusing it from a tree-top."

"There may be just a shadow of truth in that," said Mr. Squirrel, who was nothing if not broad-minded in matters of this sort.

"Fiddle-sticks," said Mrs. Squirrel.

"Scolds," muttered Grizzle. "Ever heard Mrs. Mac-Doodle talking to the Reverend Ebenezer when he forgot to post that letter and walked into Blink Bonnie without wiping his muddy boots on the door-mat? If you haven't, my boy, you've got something to learn about the art of scolding. Ever heard the humans at election-time, explaining how they love one another? Why, I've sat quivering like an aspen-leaf only to hear the sound of their scolding, not to speak of understanding it."

"What else does the wise human say?" asked Mrs. Squirrel. "I *do* think it's amusing."

"He says that Red Squirrels have acquired a very bad reputation as compared with Grey Squirrels," continued Solo.

"On what grounds, may I ask?" said Mr. Squirrel with some asperity. He was very proud of the fine color for which he had been named *Rufus*.

"Why, he says that Red Squirrels sometimes eat birds' eggs."

"Well! I'm derned!" said Grandfather Grizzle. "*What* does the Reverend Ebenezer MacDoodle have every mornin' for his breakfast? He has eggs biled. He has eggs fried. He has eggs poached. He has eggs scrambled. He has eggs with his bacon. He has eggs with his kidneys. He has eggs with his sausages. He has eggs with tomatoes; he has eggs with French Fried. He has eggs *à la Russe!* He has eggs *à la Prusse!* He has omelets of eggs; he has eggs and dried haddock; and, when he has a cold in his fat head, he has a thing called an egg-nog, with sherry in it. Not content with this he has . . ."

"Dear Papa," interrupted Mrs. Squirrel, "pray don't agitate yourself. I really do think these humans are *most* amusing."

"So do I," said Solo. "But the author goes further than that. He says that Squirrels sometimes display bloodthirsty instincts and devour young birds."

Grandfather Grizzle rose from his place in the chimney-corner. He no longer pretended to be "tough."

"Birds," he said, in a low quivering voice. "And a

human said it; a human in cold print has the nerve to use that language about Squirrels, in cold print, for . . . occasionally lunching upon a bird. Will you very kindly go into the kitchen, and bring me the *Boston* Cookery Book. Not the New York Cookery Book, or the Chicago Cookery Book! We know what to expect from *them*. I want only the *Boston* Cookery Book."

Solo was so impressed by the old gentleman's manner that he laid down his pencil and paper and obeyed. It was a fat brown quarto, with illustrations; and it was, of course, these illustrations that had risen so ironically in Grizzle's mind. Solo laid it on the floor before him.

"Thank you," said Grizzle, with a polite bow. He waited for a moment to set his thoughts in order. Then he made the following little speech.

"The Squirrels," he said, "are accused in cold print by the humans, of having bloodthirsty instincts, because they have been known to enjoy a young bird for luncheon. Personally, as you know, I am a vegetarian; and all our family here are vegetarians. But I do not wish to suggest that other Squirrels may not have other tastes. I want to call your attention to certain facts about the humans, and their treatment of birds. The Reverend Ebenezer MacDoodle of Blink Bonnie has what he calls a hen-house, with a wire cage attached to it. In this cage he keeps a large number of birds which he deliberately fattens for his own dinner. He also eats turkeys, ducks, geese, pigeons, partridges, quail and grouse. Will you, Solo, now kindly oblige the blood-thirsty Squirrels, by reading from the cookery book the interesting description of the treatment accorded to birds, after their necks have been wrung by the more civilized hands of the humans. You will find some cold print, I believe, immediately opposite the revolting picture, in the exact middle of the book. Yes. That's it."

Solo picked up the book and began to read:

"To clean giblets, cut fat from gizzard. Make a gash through thickest part of gizzard . . ."

Curly stuck her fingers into her ears.

"Stop," she cried, "stop!"

"You see," said Grizzle. "It is really a little too much for the bloodthirsty Squirrels. You needn't read further, Solo. I will only add that, on the next page, there is an interesting picture illustrating the use of skewers."

"What are skewers?" asked Ruff.

"Skewers are things that the gentle humans stick through birds," said Grizzle, "after they've done those other things to them. I've seen a female human with a dead bird skewered to her hat; and those are the folk who accuse us Squirrels of . . ." He broke off, and went back to his chimney-corner.

"It's bad," said Mrs. Squirrel.

"It's very bad," said Ruff and Curly.

"It's incredible," said Mr. Squirrel.

"It's true," said Solo, "and what's more, they do it to

one another, and worse. Humans have roasted humans alive."

They all looked quickly up at Solo. Was this what they had been trying to do to *him?*

"They don't always do it with fire," he added.

Curly's eyes had been fixed on Solo for some time and, as they were very innocent eyes, they often saw more than others.

"Poor Solo," she said, quietly, almost as if she knew exactly what the humans had been trying to do to him. Grandfather Grizzle, too, was looking at him with the curious anxiety of affection, which showed itself also in a little grunt of sympathy, saying more kindly than words could have done, "What's on your mind, Solo, my lad?"

Then, suddenly, Solo put his head in his hands, and bowed it down between his knees, as if he were going to weep. He didn't. He raised it again, almost as quickly, and very proudly. But Curly saw that his dark eyes were wet. The Squirrels clustered closely around him. Curly and Ruff got on to his shoulders and pressed their soft little flanks against his face. But they were not asking for anything this time. They were giving something to Solo.

"Little Squirrels," he said, as though he would have taken them all into his bursting heart, "little Squirrels, you don't know, you don't know the things that can happen among the humans."

And then he told them his trouble, not because they

could understand it, but because he had to pour it out or break his heart, and he felt that they were fond of him.

He told them of the stolen things he had found in the crow's nest, and how he had taken them back to their owners. He told them of the conversation he had overheard later, between Willard Wall and his mother, Mrs. Drew.

"I never *did* believe that cock-and-bull story about the crow taking 'em," said Willard Wall. "Solo tuk the things himself. Of course, he did. Not because he's a nateral thief, but because he's queer; and he brought 'em back because he's growin' queerer."

Mrs. Drew did not attempt to defend Solo's odd story about the crow. This was one of the things that had hurt Solo most. He was in bed at the time. The conversation took place early one morning at the door of the cottage, immediately below his window, so that although they had spoken in subdued voices, his very sharp ears heard every syllable. He did not see the white and frightened look on his mother's face, or he might have understood her inability to defend him. She really had been convinced that Solo must be queer. So many stolid blockheads had said it; and, when Willard Wall went on to more serious suggestions, her mind almost refused to work.

"Mrs. Drew," Willard Wall continued, "I'm going to tell you sumpin' I never said before. About two months ago, actin' on Mr. MacDoodle's orders, I shot a squirrel down by Blink Bonnie. It had hardly touched the ground, when this lad of yours jumps out of the bushes, grabs it with both his hands, and turns to me with his eyes blazin' like a catamount. I thought he'd a-killed me. If you'd heard what he said to me, you'd have known it wasn't safe to have him around. Folks as fierce as that ought to be locked up. It ain't good for *him;* it ain't good for *you;* and it ain't good for the village to have him growin' queerer and queerer till one of these days he'll take a knife to someone. Folks that never locked their doors before are locking them now. You ought to have him put under lock and key."

Of all this, the Squirrels understood very little except that their friend's eyes had once again the look of a hunted stag, and that he thought he was in danger of the worst thing that can happen to any creature—the loss of his freedom. It was not his words; it was his look that told them about it; and they had seen the fear growing upon him for many days past. His wish to stay this night at Blueberry Cottage suggested that some crisis was approaching; and they were glad that it was winter, and that the snow was drifted ten feet deep around their sheltering walls.

They understood one other thing—that he found comfort in their friendship, as they found happiness in his. After a while, he pulled himself together and rose to put another log on the fire.

When he came back to his drawing board he found

Ruff and Curly bent over the picture on which he had been working with colored chalks. They looked up at him with something like awe."

"It's much better than the one on the wall," said Ruff.

"Show it to Grandfather," said Curly. "I'm sure he'll like this one."

Solo chuckled and took his drawing over to the chimney-corner.

Grizzle stared at this new picture in astonishment. It was really a remarkable drawing. It depicted Grandfather Grizzle, marching in triumph at the head of his army of red ants and tossing his Michaelmas daisy into the air like the baton of a drum-major. Solo had caught the very gleam in his eye, the rakish cock of his elbows, the backward tilt of his body, and the goose-step in which he was leading his troops. You could almost hear the rhythm of the marching feet.

It wasn't only the outside of Grandfather Grizzle that you saw. It was everything he was thinking about the Porcupine, although the Porcupine wasn't in the picture at all. Very few humans could have seen that; but the Squirrels—all except Rufus—knew what he was thinking, at once, because they read each other's thoughts by a kind of wireless telegraphy.

Grizzle looked at it in blank astonishment at first. Then his mouth opened slightly. Then he chuckled; and, finally, he slapped his leg, spat his acorn plug into the fire, and remarked:

"Solo, my lad, you've done it! Derned if I don't believe you rightfully belong to the—er—"

Mrs. Squirrel hesitated. Last time, she had helped him with 'Circles'; and he had deliberately changed it to 'Chimney.' This time, therefore, she said, very quickly,

"The—er—Chimney-circles!"

Grandfather Grizzle looked at her steadily for a moment, as though he saw right through her.

"*Studio,*" he said. "Solo must have been born in a *studio* himself."

16

FATHER FRANCIS BRINGS NEWS

IT MUST HAVE BEEN midnight, or later, when the
really great surprise came. The Squirrels were
fast asleep in their down beds, while Solo, wrapped in
a rug, with his head on a cushion, lay on the floor as
near the dying fire as possible. He was not asleep. His
dark shining eyes had watched endless pictures crumbling away in the glowing embers; and when he looked
at the walls and ceiling, he had seen a hundred fantastic shadows growing and shrinking like witches, or
creeping in and out of the silver birch trellis, up the
stairs, and around the gallery, like woodland sprites.

Closing his eyes for a moment, he thought of his
beloved Pooduck Island, and that glimpse of a lovelier
sea and sky which he had caught through the gap in the
cedar wood. He always thought of that arched gap in

162

the wood as a kind of eye, through which he had been allowed to look, once. The radiant picture he had seen, and tried to paint, later, for Father Francis, would still be radiant in other summers; but its radiance, apparently, was dangerous for him. There was no unhappiness in it; but his own thoughts of it were tinged with all the deeper sense of loss. He remembered the frightened look in his mother's face when he said to her, one evening, after he had been working on the picture, *'Pooduck Island has an Eye.'* It was a queer way of talking, perhaps, unless they knew all that was in his mind. He had come back all aglow with things that he could never explain to anyone in a thousand years. The phrase he used—*Pooduck Island has an Eye*— meant something beautiful to him when he said it, and he had said it as though it were a line in some mysterious poem. Perhaps that, too, sounded frightening to her. Now, it came back to him, as if the very stillness of the snow-hushed woods outside were solemnly warning him that nobody must speak or think like that. He seemed to hear a mysterious voice completing the poem inside his own head. It was a voice of infinite sadness breathing its music into his troubled brain from a world beyond our world. It was the same voice that had gone through the autumn woods, two months ago, echoing the song of Silly James; the same voice that had sung of the Squirrel corn and the little brown Indian. But tonight it was a silent voice, in his own heart and mind, and there would be no footprints in the deep muffling whiteness of the world outside. It could never be put into words; but, if it could, this is what it seemed to say:

> Pooduck Island has an Eye,
> Ne'er look through it!
> 'Ware that lovelier sea and sky
> Or you'll rue it.

> Eye that in a little wood,
> Boughs all round it,
> Opens on a world as good
> As youth found it.

> Window in a world of pain!
> Up, lad, flee it;
> Lest your heaven be born again,
> And you see it.

> Birds and men that once had wings
> And have lost them
> Know (with those who see such things)
> All it cost them.

He had closed his eyes for a minute or two when there came a sharp knocking at the shutter of the window by which he had entered the cottage. The knocking was undoubtedly human; and Solo was on his feet instantly, with the alertness of a wild creature. They must be on his track already, he thought; and, as he stood, holding his breath to listen, he could hear the thumping of his own heart.

After a pause, the knocking at the shutter was re-peated more loudly. Solo stood quite still, waiting, till he heard a hand fumbling with the catch and trying to pull the shutter back. At this, he moved, swiftly, on tiptoe, to the back of the room and crept into the large cubbyhole under the stairs. The door of this fitted so closely into the paneling of the staircase that it had a good chance of escaping detection altogether. There was a knot-hole in front through which he caught the gleam of the hearth, and could watch the intruder; and if he, or they, went to search the kitchen or the floor above, Solo thought he could then escape by the window.

He had hardly hidden himself before the shutter rattled back, and the window went up. Through the black opening came the head and shoulders of a man wearing a high fur cap, thick blue scarf and heavy coat. He did not seem to be an experienced burglar, and made several somewhat clumsy attempts before he suc-ceeded in getting the rest of his body through the win-dow. The room was very dark, for the firelight was only flickering now; and it was not till the strange visitor stood in front of the hearth, and clicked his tongue with astonishment at the sight of the fire that Solo recognized Father Francis.

Solo himself was so astonished at this that he kept quite still in his hiding place at first. He saw Father Francis pick up the drawing of Grandfather Grizzle at the head of his red ant army. Father Francis looked very grave indeed as he examined this. He took an electric torch out of his pocket and pored over it, making curious little exclamations and whistling sounds. He shook his head very seriously as he laid it down. It looked as if the best of Solo's human friends had now concluded that the red ant drawing was the final evidence against him. It was only in the kindness of his heart that the old padre had been humoring him, and pretending that he was all right. Solo felt that he might as well face it. The old padre called up the stair, "Solo! Come down! I want to see you! It's Father Francis. I've something very important to tell you!" He called rather loudly, as if he thought Solo would be sleeping in the best bedroom; Solo startled him very much indeed by answering through a knot-hole, about three inches from the padre's nose, "I'm here, Father. I'll be with you, at once."

Very queer indeed was the conversation that followed.

"Solo, my lad," said the old man, "you shouldn't have done this. You really shouldn't. I've been looking everywhere for you."

"Done what?" said Solo rather fiercely.

Father Francis laid both his hands on Solo's shoulders, and looked steadily into his dark smouldering eyes.

"You've done nothing that you were accused of; but it might have been a serious mistake to come here."

"Who told you I was here?"

"Nobody told me. There was no way of tracing you in the daytime. But turning your snowshoes back to front is a very old trick; so, at last, with the help of what you told me yourself about your little friends, the Squirrels—well, here I am!"

"Nobody else knows?" asked Solo. "They wanted to shut me up in one of those awful places. You haven't told anyone?"

The padre looked at him, and Solo understood.

"All the same you shouldn't have come here," said Father Francis. "You could have come to *my* house; and we would soon have put an end to all this nonsense about shutting you up. The days have gone by when the crazy people could shut up the sane people as easily as that."

"Maybe," said Solo. "But those days are coming back. I feel it in my bones. We're all being tied up in knots, so that we can't do anything about it. There's too much telling everyone how they have to live, and what they must think, and how they must tie their boot-laces. They turn little knobs, and listen to it every night, till they can't think any more for themselves; and they want to shut up anybody who does."

"Too many Burrow Cats," said a queer little drowsy voice, from the chimney-corner. It was Grandfather Grizzle, talking in his sleep. To Father Francis, it was just a squirrel's drowsy chirrup. But Solo understood it, and a smile flitted across his brooding face.

"Well—that's true enough," said Father Francis, answering Solo, not Grizzle, "but you're safe enough now, my lad. I've something very serious to tell you."

He hesitated, because he wanted to break the news in the way that would help Solo most.

"It's possible," he went on, "that you have been kept away from the world, in this quiet little village, for a great purpose . . . The picture you painted for me, *Pooduck Island has an Eye*—you remember you told me I could do what I liked with it? Well—I sent it to New York."

"To New York," cried Solo. "What has New York got to do with Pooduck Island? I wanted *you* to keep it!"

"*Mea culpa*," said Father Francis. "If I had kept it, I might have paid off the entire debt on the village church and made all the necessary improvements, too. I believe we might even have bought that organ . . ." He loved music, and "that organ," as he called it, had been one of his great renunciations.

It was Solo's turn now to look at Father Francis with alarm. Nothing that Solo ever said had sounded quite as crazy as this.

"I heard this morning," Father Francis continued, "that *Pooduck Island has an Eye* was just queer enough, and beautiful enough, to convince the critics you are an artist, Solo. It has been accepted for exhibition at the big show this winter; and the judges were so interested in its 'queerness' that two of the chief art galleries in the United States want to add it to their permanent collection of queernesses."

His face became grave again.

"You know what this means, Solo. It means a big change in your life, my lad."

"Why?" said Solo.

"I hope it won't change *you* too much," said Father Francis, "but, in outside things, it will make a big change. It means that you'll be famous. I wonder what fame really tastes like?"

"Mud, I should think," said Solo. "Anyway, I don't want it. I painted that picture for you."

"It means that you've arrived," said Father Francis.

"Where?" said Solo.

"Ah," said Father Francis, "that *is* the question. But they call it arriving. Very often it means departing. However, they are all saying that *the ball is at your feet.*"

"What ball?" said Solo.

"That thing," said Father Francis, flashing his electric torch on a terrestrial globe in a corner.

"It's dusty," said Solo. "I'd much rather have Pooduck Island or Blueberry Cottage."

"You can have them, if you like," said Father Francis, growing noticeably queerer every minute. "You're rich already, comparatively speaking."

"Rich," cried Solo, who had long been wondering how he was to buy some more painting materials. He explained that he wanted brushes, tubes of color, all kinds of things.

"I think you're rich enough for that," said Father Francis.

"Rich enough to buy an easel?" asked Solo.

"*Pooduck Island has an Eye* won the Hartman Prize," said Father Francis. "The press wasn't much interested in what *you* saw; but it tumbled over itself about that Eye; and, as a result, there are two great galleries in the market for that picture, each of them empowered to pay for it out of their endowment. As neither of them could beat the other, a private citizen in each of the two cities came forward, and—in patriotic rivalry, no less than in admiration for your painting—they've bid it up to four times the amount. It now goes to the Redman Gallery."

"And where do *I* go?" asked Solo. "County Lunatic Asylum? What will Mrs. Wall say?"

Father Francis laughed.

"I've some news for you about that, too. I hope it will relieve your mind. If I hadn't been anxious about your disappearance, I should have spent most of the day laughing. She has now lost the little gold watch which belonged to her great grandmother. Perhaps you didn't know that when you pinched it."

Solo himself couldn't help smiling at this.

"I suppose she really does think I did it!" he exclaimed.

"She implored you to bring it back to her," chuckled

Father Francis. "But she doesn't think you took it, or the other stuff any more. She thinks you are the only person who knows where it is. Yesterday afternoon Mrs. Wall took the watch out of its drawer for an important purpose. She had decided to boil an egg for her tea, and the clock in the kitchen had stopped dead, owing to a broken spring. These details I find fascinating, Solo. They show the very careful way in which events are brought about by the imps or angels who take care of folk like you. Mrs. Wall took the watch —with the long gold chain—and laid it down on the kitchen-dresser to time the boiling of the egg. The kitchen-dresser stands almost up against the door; and it was on the end nearest to the door that Mrs. Wall laid the watch; so that, if the door were opened, would be almost in the open air, or—at any rate—shining gloriously in the afternoon sun."

"I begin to see," said Solo, with a broad grin.

"Wait a minute," said Father Francis. "At this very moment, however, the postman went by; and Mrs. Wall ran out after him with a letter which she urgently desired to catch the mail. Now—mark this, Solo—*the letter was to her mother, telling her how you had embarked on a career of crime, and were about to be taken away and locked up.* In her hurry to catch the mail she left the kitchen-door wide open. She delivered her letter to the postman, and was trotting back to her open door, to prevent the canary being frozen to death, when she *saw—*"

"No!" cried Solo.

"Yes!" cried Father Francis. 'She *saw, with her own eyes*—a big black *Crow*. It swooped down from the old elm, across the road, right on to the corner of the dresser which stuck out so invitingly in the doorway. Mrs. Wall saw this blessed bird pick up a bright object on the dresser. She saw the gold chain dangling from its claws and glittering in the sun. She saw the Crow backing up and out with one mighty flap of its wings; and then she sat helplessly down in a damp snow-drift, and saw the dirty black thief walloping away to the ends of the earth, and making a bee-line for the moon beyond the water."

"I'll never say anything against crows again," said Solo, doubling up with a sudden spasm of laughter.

"Nor I," said Father Francis. "An hour later Mrs. Wall came to see me. She implored me to use my influence with *you* to get her treasure back. I reminded her of certain things and said you weren't likely to be in the mood for helping her. 'If he doesn't, I'll have the law of him,' she said; 'for he knows where that crow has taken it.' 'Mrs. Wall,' I said to her, very solemnly, 'you said yourself that you were going to have him locked up for saying that very thing.' 'Ah well,' she said, 'we must let bygones be bygones. I'll compensate him for the little unpleasantness. I'll give him a nice new paint-box, so that he can amuse himself harmlessly with his daubs and smudges for the next twelve months.' It was then I showed her the letter from the Art Committee in New York. "Who's wrong in the head, now, Mrs. Wall?' I asked her. 'Why, I suppose it's New York,' she said. 'However, if I get my watch back, I'll apologize. But don't let the village know I've apologized, or they'll laugh at me.' I thought this was very bad, so I said again, rather sternly: '*Laugh at you indeed, I should think they will!*' I'd no sooner said it than a loon down by the shore began to laugh. It sounded like a whole village of crazy hobgoblins all laughing at once. It echoed and echoed and echoed, and it ended with a hoot that just curdled your blood. It was the finishing touch for Mrs. Willard Wall. 'Oh!' she gasped, 'how awful!' She gave me one horror-stricken look and went as white as a blanc-mange. 'How dare you?' she said. You see, poor dear, she really *did* think I'd been calling up Imps from the Pit. Then—I'm afraid *I* began to laugh. I couldn't resist it. The look on her face as she sidled out of my door, keeping one eye on me over her shoulder, has been haunting me all day, and making me laugh at the wrong time, in the most alarming manner. I'm sure my housekeeper thinks I've gone quite crazy. She asked me if I would have a fried sole for my breakfast tomorrow morning, and I began to laugh like an idiot. I think we must forgive Mrs. Wall."

"I think we must get Mrs. Wall's watch back for her tomorrow," said Solo. "But what do you want me to do now?"

"I want you to come back to my house," said Father Francis. "We'll talk about the rest in the morning."

It was a wonderful walk they had, through the white hushed woods that night. It was only a week before Christmas, and the skies were crowded with stars that seemed to know it. As Father Francis and Solo went up the sleeping village street, some of the little Christmas trees which, according to the local custom, were set outside the cottages, were still carrying tiny gold and crimson stars of their own, which cast a curious unearthly glow over the green boughs. A few yards from the padre's house, Solo said to him, "You must have wondered, sometimes, if they weren't right about me."

They were just at the door of the village church as he said it. Father Francis laid a hand upon his arm and said quietly, "Come and see."

He pushed back the door through which anyone could enter. He turned on a light or two, and led the way up the dim aisle to the kindly glow where a few candles were still burning before the statue of Our Lady. She was looking gently down at the crib where the dumb creatures were gathered about the Child in the straw. Around her neck, resting on her breast, and apparently clasped in her right hand, hung the Indian rosary of shells. The colors had never looked so beautiful. No pearls had ever glowed with so lovely a light.

"That is where I put your gift on the night when you gave it to me," said Father Francis, "and it has remained there."

17

JACOPONO AGAIN

A SONG-SPARROW piped five happy notes where the pines went down to the sunlit wash of the sea. Solo turned from his easel and looked through the open door of the studio . . . listening. He heard the answering cry, an elfin echo, dying away in the lonely forest, as he had heard it from childhood. It was not meant to be wasted—that song *keen and sweet as a pine-needle, pricking your heart.* . . . Perhaps, after all, somebody *was* there. Perhaps, after all, Solo was the one who was meant to hear it.

He went back to his easel, and began to paint again. But he was not alone. Grandfather Grizzle sat on the arm of the old oak chair behind him, chewing his plug of acorn and watching, with a curious excitement, the mysterious growth of the new picture.

From time to time Grandfather Grizzle would make a remark which to others might seem only the chirrup of a contented Squirrel, though Solo understood it perfectly. For instance, at this actual moment, Grizzle was saying, "Guess you like this a lot better than Noo York, eh Solo?" And Solo gave only a quiet little grunt in reply. But Grizzle understood *him* equally well, and continued,

"Glad to know Blueberry Cottage is your property now, Solo. I reckon your mother likes it too, eh?"

"Uh-huh."

Solo was too intensely rapt in his picture for more; but, between friends, "uh-huh" can speak whole encyclopedias. So Grizzle chirped happily on.

" 'Snice place! My family enjoyed bein' there very much this winter. All out in the woods now, of course, for the summer. Had a nice little breckfuss with 'em 'smornin'. Fresh mushrooms, and crisp young maple-buds. Tasted fine after all that dry winter-food. Ever tried squirrel-corn, Solo?"

"No, what's that?"

"Grows down by Blink Bonnie. It's a root; but it carries little flowers that tell you just where to dig, by their scent. It's a bit like wild roses, only more delicate. And the roots are just little knobs of the tenderest and milkiest corn y'ever tasted. Delicious."

"That so?"

"Ought to try it, some day."

"P'raps I will."

"Reckon you must ha' talked to Willard Wall 'bout that shootin'. He don't interfere with us Squirrels any more, down by Blink Bonnie. How come that, Solo?"

"Well. Mrs. Willard Wall had some trouble with her kitchen-clock. Had to use her best watch when she was boiling eggs. That's how she pretty nearly lost it to that old crow. So I gave her a nice new cuckoo-clock."

"What's that, Solo?"

"Bird comes out of a little door every hour, and shouts *cuckoo* at her. But she likes it. It's too big for any crow to fly away with it. When I got her watch back, I made a sort of agreement. No more shooting Squirrels in these woods. All they've got to do is to make Blink Bonnie squirrel-tight; and, as I told them, you'll have your room at Blueberry Cottage now."

"What about Mrs. MacDoodle's fur coat?"

"It's going to be Skunk, now."

"Tha's good. Say, Solo. There ain't no chance, I s'pose, of these humans turnin' *you* out of Blueberry Cottage an' the *Circles*, seeing as you bought 'em out of your own paint-box. I mean, you only gev a picture for 'em, didn't you?"

Solo grinned.

"Never know what humans may do," he said.

"Ah!" Grandfather Grizzle ejaculated, looking anxious. "Have they brought you any of them forms to fill up yet?"

"Three, this morning."

"Ah. Thought as much. Too many Burrow Cats. Many questions on the forms?"

"I can only count up to ten. But there were lots of tens."

"Ah. I was afraid of that," said Grizzle, wrinkling his nose, and looking very anxious indeed. "Hope they don't turn you out, Solo."

"Well, Grizzle, until they do, we've fixed up a loft for the Squirrel family, whenever you want to come back; and we've made a special door for you that no weasels or owls, or martins, or minks could ever wangle. It'll be fun round the fire, next winter.

"Now, Grandfather," said Solo, "I want you to help me with this picture."

Grandfather Grizzle tried to be modest. "You've learned all I can teach you, Solo," he said. "You're in the Circles yourself now."

"All the same, I want your help," said Solo. "I want to get the whole Squirrel family into this picture, and I can't do that unless you find them for me."

Grandfather Grizzle went to the door and gave a clear chirruping whistle, which was answered by four others; and, almost at once, Mr. and Mrs. Squirrrel, Ruff, and Curly, appeared on the threshold.

"Will you all please follow me," said Solo.

He picked up his easel and carried it out to the clearing which overlooked the sea; then he went back for the other things he needed. When he was ready he pointed to an old tree-stump in the middle of the clearing and said, "We'll have to make that do for Jacopono, at present. I want Grizzle to be at his feet on the left, and Rufus on the right. Ruff and Curly on those broken boughs which must do for his shoulders; and Cosy just there, in the crook of his arm. No. Not facing me. I want you all to turn your backs to me and look out across the water to Pooduck Island." They obeyed him; but Grandfather Grizzle felt he ought to point one thing out.

"I've only one criticism, so far," said Grizzle. "I really do believe it's usual, Solo, to paint the front view of folks, in an important family portrait like this."

"It's different when you are painting folks who can talk with their tails," said Solo, with a grin.

So there they sat, all five of them, giving a fine back view of themselves, silhouetted in dark umber against the opalescent sea.

One or another of them, from time to time, would make a remark over the shoulder to their queer friend, the artist; but he was too busy to say very much in reply. Pooduck Island, across the water, was growing black against the sunset, and so were the Squirrels, before the sitting came to an end.

"I wish it was Jacopono's own shoulders we'd been sitting on," said Ruff.

"So do I," said Curly.

"We never found out who made those footprints," said Ruff, "or who it was that went through the wood that night, singing."

"Did *you* ever find out, Solo?" said Grizzle.

"Didn't need to find out," said Solo. "I *knew*."

"*Knew,*" said all the Squirrels together.

"I've often heard him singing," said Solo. "You might think it was the wind in the pines, or the waves on the beach. But I can usually tell. He's in the picture now. Come and see, if you really want to know what he looks like."

The two young Squirrels leapt down, with Cosy, from their perch on the old tree-stump, which was pretending to be Jacopono; and all five of them clustered eagerly round Solo to look at the picture. Ruff and Curly, of course, took the best seats, on his shoulders.

It was magic. He had got it all in: Pooduck Island darkening against the west; the opalescent sea; and, in the foreground, the meadow-clearing with the clusters of soft white flowers, which, in the strange old folk-name, are called "life everlasting." In the center of the meadow-clearing the whole Squirrel family were clustered—as they had been directed—on the old tree-stump. But it was no longer a tree-stump. It was Jacopono himself sitting on the tree-stump; and it wasn't the ancient Jacopono; it was a Jacopono of the Maine woods, who had lived among the Indians, and wore sandals of deer-skin.

He had made that rosary of wampum for the broken-hearted wife of the Sagamore, whose little son had been flung into the river and drowned. In the picture the softly luminous chain hung over his left arm, and all the opalescence of the sea was repeated and focused into the lovely forms and colors of the shells. His face was turned towards the Squirrel in the crook of his arm, so that you could see he was full of kindness. But the light on his face was far more beautiful than the Squirrels could understand. It came from the after-glow in the sky.

His right hand was pointing to the Island across the water. He seemed to be telling them he was going to the place where the world ends; and, a little way below, on the beach, waiting to go with him in search of the little brown son and the Indian mother, stood the shadowy figure of the Sagamore by his birch canoe.

They all looked, for some time, in silence. It was not like looking at a picture. It was like looking through a window—at something real that was also a great mystery; and the lapping of the waves on the shore might have been the lapping of the waves against the bow of the birch-canoe; but Jacopono belonged to the mystery.

"Did he come out of the wood, when our backs were turned," whispered Curly, whose little heart was beating to think it was she who lay there in the crook of his arm. "You must have seen him, or he couldn't have crept into the picture like that!"

"Ss-h!" said Solo. "Listen! He's just stealing away through the wood."

It was all so still that, in the silence between the wash of the waves, they heard a twig snapping a hundred yards away among the pines. Then, as quietly as the sunset wind comes through the treetops, they heard the same voice, in an echo of a lovelier song, dying farther and farther away:

Squirrel-corn, squirrel-corn,—youth and the sweet
    of it!
Dig for the root, little Indian, and eat of it.
Gather the sweet grass and make you a nest of it.
Mother and little brown son have the best of it!

Happy their hunting-ground, bright with the flower
    of it!
Theirs was the kingdom, once; ay, and the power
    of it!
Where are they flown, then?—O, swift as the swallow,
Sagamore, dip your dark paddle and follow.

THE END

DATE DUE

GAYLORD			PRINTED IN U.S.A